Summer of the Suffragists

of the

Gayle Eggen Aanensen

CONTENTS

Acknowledgements

I dedicate this second book in a series of historical fiction with love to husband, Ted, for supporting my efforts totally, from the "big picture" all the way down to scanning and sending illustrations.

Much to my surprise, I've discovered my muse is actually Ocean Grove, the little seaside town in N.J., known since 1869 as "God's Square Mile." As a child with roaming parents who moved incessantly, I had no clear sense of "home" or "setting"—a valuable tool for most authors. I'm grateful to finally land on a piece of geography that feeds my creative soul.

Once again I thank the Historical Society of Ocean Grove for its wealth of information, pictures, and post cards, especially Harriet Russomano and Herb Bachmann. Another member, Mary Solecki, arranged for students at Carl Sandburg Middle School to read two chapters of the early manuscript. Five students in Kathy Fischer's English class gave such enthusiastic, intelligent critiques that I fully expect to read their own books someday!

To my friends in the Tri-Muse writing group, thank you for sticking with me through two-plus years of writing and rewriting. I wish us all success as we grow into an expanded group, Jersey Shore Writers. My thanks also to shopkeeper Terry Lepore of "Gingerbreads" for the beautiful cover image; and to author Helen Pike, whose memoir-writing class helped me find the "voice" for this book.

Many thanks to our three grown children, Matt (and Rose), Greta (and Sandy), and Tim for their advice and support. I especially thank mother-in-law Gladys, Ted, and Greta for reading the entire manuscript. And hugs and kisses to granddaughter Madeleine, always.

For more information on the early 20th century era, see the "Resources" page at the end of the book. And please visit my website www.GayleEggenAanensen.com

CHAPTER ONE

The Getaway

Tent life in Ocean Grove

Mama and I stood on the platform at Grand Central Terminal like lost islands in a surging sea of travelers. People ebbed and flowed around us, dragging luggage and children as they waited for the train to the New Jersey seashore resorts. The clang and clamor of construction echoed through the building and banged against my ears.

"Porter!" yelled a man in a black suit. "Over here!" He

sat on his wooden steamer trunk and wiped the sweat from his face. His wife balanced a baby on one hip and two hat boxes on the other. The baby began to cry.

Two boys raced by, nearly knocking me over. "William! George!" scolded a woman in a plain black dress, clearly a nanny. "Come back here." She chased after the boys, her face as shiny and red as an apple. Porters blew their whistles, herding the crowd toward the track. Children laughed, mothers scolded, and a man nearby snapped his pocket watch open and shut, open and shut.

Only Mama and I stood motionless, worn out from the terrible fight with Father. We carried nothing—nothing visible anyway—but I'd wager my heart was as heavy as any of these fully-packed trunks. Even now, with all these people and all this noise, the image of my parents' fight ran through my head over and over, like the moving pictures on a nickelodeon at Coney Island. And I couldn't stop putting in nickels.

I saw Father coming home early. Too early. And drunk. Mama begging him not to go to the saloon tomorrow. Pleading for him to bring home his full week's pay.

Father slapping her hard in the face. Twice. Her terrified screams.

"Run, Mother!" I'd yelled.

"That's right, Fannie," Father had growled. "Get out! I'm sick of your nagging. But Elsie stays." He grabbed my arm and gripped it with the same strength he used swinging a pick-axe underground. He smashed an empty liquor bottle on the stone sink with his other hand.

"I can't leave you, Elsie," Mama cried, stepping forward.

"Get back!" I screamed. Too late. Father lunged, aiming the jagged bottle at Mama's face. Instinctively, her hand flew up, and the glass ripped into her palm. Blood dripped to the floor. Father dropped the bottle and staggered backwards. "No, no, no," he moaned. He loosened his grip. I broke free.

"Let's go, Mama. Run!" I threw a dishtowel over her hand, pushed her out the door, and we flew down the stairs. The O'Brien twins were counting marbles on a landing. "Look out," I yelled, as we raced around them. Grandma O'Brien was sitting outside the tenement on the front stoop. Her eyes opened wide, and I knew she'd spread the story of our escape quicker than a newsboy. We jumped on the trolley and rode to the train station. The last few coins in Mama's pocket bought tickets, and here we waited.

"All aboard for New Jersey seashore resorts," called the conductor. I followed Mama as she dragged herself up the iron steps. We watched from our window as a pair of muscular, bare-armed men hoisted trunk after trunk onto the train.

"Your father digs in the pit somewhere around here," Mama said. "For the new Grand Central Station. He said it'll be the wonder of the modern world. Said it was killing him." Her voice trailed away.

Passengers swept into our car, looking for seats. Many smiled, but their eyes shifted away from Mama's bruised face and bloody towel. We were not a story they wished to hear as they began their summer holidays.

I read my wrinkled ticket once again. "TO LONG BRANCH, N.J." was at the top. Below that, "From New

York City," and finally, "Good for One Passage This Day and This Train Only." It might as well have said, "No Return Ever to Your Drunken Father." I turned the ticket over. The back was stamped, "Wednesday, July 5, 1905." One day before my thirteenth birthday.

"Rest while you can, Elsie," Mama said. "I didn't have enough money to get us all the way to Ocean Grove. We'll have to get off at Long Branch and walk. A couple miles, at least." She leaned her head back and closed her eyes.

How could she sleep? I wondered. I was wide awake, my head spinning with questions. How long would we live in Grandfather's tent? What would we do in the winter? What about my clothes? What about school? And Molly? Molly with the golden braids and infectious laugh. I missed my best friend already.

The train clanged its bell and chugged into motion. Mama's head rolled side to side. We picked up speed, the wheels clackety-clacking loudly. Coal smoke blew in the open window. Its stench, and the rocking motion of the train, churned my stomach into a nauseous stew, as if I'd eaten spoiled meat. I swallowed over and over to keep the bile from rising up and spewing onto my lap. Mama was smart. I closed my eyes.

I must have dozed, because the sun was setting when the train slowed. "Long Branch!" called the conductor. One long screech and the train stopped. We stepped off.

"How many miles to Ocean Grove?" Mama asked a porter.

"A little over seven miles, ma'm, but not quite eight.

May I get you a carriage?"

"No," Mama said, without explanation. She turned her back on the golden sunset and walked east, toward the ocean. A sudden wave of fresh salt air revived me. I breathed it in deeply, like a bellows, pushing the coal smoke from my lungs.

The swampy salt marsh smell grew stronger as we walked. It tickled my nose and jolted my memory back to long-ago visits with my grandparents. One whiff of the ocean and my heart felt lighter. My head clearer. Suddenly I remembered running in and out of the waves, holding hands with my parents, the three of us carefree and laughing. We marked the wet sand with our footprints, and watched the waves sweep them away. I became that little girl again, smelling the salty air and feeling it blow through my hair. I wanted to throw open my arms, twirl and dance, and leave footprints in the sand.

Mama stumbled beside me. I grabbed her elbow and slowed my pace. There would be no dancing tonight. It was dark when we reached the beach. I barely heard Mama over the crashing waves. "What did you say?" I yelled.

"I need to rest. My rib hurts. Let's sit on the sand." We sat, and she slumped against me. I put my arm around her.

"I'm sorry, Mama. Can I help you?"

"Yes. Wet my towel, please. The salt water will clean the cut." I dipped the towel in the cold sea and wrung it out. She wrapped it around her hand, hissing as salt stung the wound. "You were smart to throw me the towel,

Elsie. Quick-thinking. But then, you've always been like that."

"Wish I'd grabbed a sweater too," I said. "It's chilly. How will we get our clothes, Mama?"

"I don't know, Elsie. But we can't go home. There won't even be a home if your father doesn't pay the landlord this week. It's our last chance. But he'll drink away his pay tomorrow; I know he will! I...I can't talk anymore. I need my strength for walking. Help me up, please."

We found a road and walked south, silent and slow. The crescent moon hung like a smile in the sky, keeping us company. I heard a carriage behind us, the clip-clop of the horse's hooves getting louder and louder. Mama slipped back on the sand, out of sight. "I don't want to answer anybody's questions," she said, "or take anyone's charity." It was the same when we heard the rattle of a motor car.

"Look at the round headlamps, Mama. Don't they look like tiny full moons, shining on the street?"

"That's my daughter, the poet. You see things differently, Elsie. I see rich people in a fancy, open air motor car, returning to their mansion on the dunes after a gay supper party. Four or five courses of delicious food. Music. Maybe dancing. How nice for them. You, my little poet, see tiny moons." A woman's laughter trailed behind the car as it disappeared in the darkness ahead.

Mama liked calling me her poet, but I couldn't rhyme for anything. Tiny moons and what? Shiny spoons? Ridiculous! Still, it made me smile as we walked and walked and walked. We passed a lake and came to a boardwalk.

"We're in Asbury Park," Mama murmured. My legs

trembled as we stumbled on, past dark, shuttered shops and another, smaller lake. Finally, Mama read a white sign, "Welcome to Ocean Grove, A Methodist-Episcopal Camp Meeting Association."

"Thank God!" Mama exclaimed. "We're safe." My legs folded like a grasshopper's and I sank down on the board-walk. "No sitting yet," Mama said. "We've got to find your grandfather's tent. It's somewhere in the middle of town, near a patch of scrub pines." We left the boardwalk a few blocks later. I followed Mama as she pushed through pitch-black tree branches, the white towel on her hand leading the way like a tiny, flickering ghost. We emerged into a clearing. Rows of dark canvas tents stretched in all directions. Gas streetlamps cast a dim light. Bells tolled from an unseen church. I counted them—twelve. It was midnight.

"Oh, there are so many more tents than I remem-bered," she sobbed. "I won't be able to find Papa's, and I can't take one more step."

"Don't worry, Mama. We'll sleep right here." I pushed pine needles into a pile and pulled her down. She groaned as she stretched out on the prickly bed. I snuggled my back against her warm body, and she fell asleep without even saying her prayers. The black sky, sprinkled with thousands of stars, made me feel very small. Just one soon-to-be-thirteen-year-old girl in a big world that didn't care if I was tired or hungry or homeless. Didn't care that my mother was hurt and my father a drunk. I said prayers for all three of us. The wind blew through the trees, whispering: sleep, sleep. So I did.

Hours later I dreamed it was Christmas. Mama and I were decorating a little pine tree. Father watched. Mama dropped a red glass ball, and it smashed into tiny red bits at her feet. Father laughed, loud and mocking. He squeezed my arm until it hurt. His breath reeked of chewing tobacco and whiskey. "No, no, no," I cried in the dream. "I want to smell the Christmas tree. Only the tree." I leaned into the tree, breathing deeply. Now I smelled pine again. No, wait. I really, really smelled it! My eyes flew open and stared up into real pine branches. I jumped to my feet.

"Good morning, Elsie Sunshine," Mama said, as if this were any ordinary day. She sat on the ground, picking pine needles from her light brown hair, streaked with gold by the rising sun. "Look at that beautiful sky," she said, "and listen, you can hear the ocean. A new day..."

And my birthday, I started to say, but one look at her swollen purple eye silenced me. I felt like crying. How could Father have done this? I laid my head in her lap.

"Oh, Elsie." She pulled her fingers through my morning hair, a frizzy tangle of mud-brown curls. "Don't worry," she said. "Everything will be fine."

After a while, a milk wagon, pulled by an old skin-and-bones horse, rolled past. We followed it down a street of sand-colored canvas tents. The milk man deposited bottles of fresh milk at several tents, picking up the empty bottles in return. I licked my dry lips. The smell of bacon and eggs and coffee wafted from the tents, igniting a firestorm in my empty stomach. I needed Grandfather, and breakfast, right now! I saw an old man pumping water from a well. He had a gray beard, just like Grandfather. It was...him! He looked exactly as I remembered.

"Grandfather!" I yelled. He raised his head.

"What?" he said, looking confused. "Elsie? Elsie, is that you? And Fannie?" I ran into his arms and buried my face in his beard. It smelled the same—a mix of cherry pipe tobacco and musty canvas. Only now, Grandfather didn't kneel down to hug me. I was nearly as tall as he was.

"Elsie, how big you are!" he exclaimed. "And Fannie. I've been thinking about you so much. How's my girl?" He reached for Mama, who chose that moment to push her hair away from her eye. Grandfather stumbled backwards, his mouth open. "What's happened, Fannie? It's Horace again, right? That no-good son of a...." He picked up his water bucket. "Come inside. We'll talk in my tent."

He pulled back the flap and I walked into a surprisingly all-white room. The morning sun shone through the canvas walls, whitewashing them bright and clean. Tom Sawyer couldn't have done it better.

Grandfather's cot and trunk were on one side. A small table with two chairs, a standing lamp and a rocking chair filled the other side. His small kitchen was in the wooden cabin built onto the back wall. It reminded me of Molly's dollhouse—a wood-burning stove, oak ice box, table, wash basin and storage shelves—all tiny and tidy. He poured two cups of coffee and stirred a pot of oatmeal, simmering on the stove. I could have eaten it right from the pot.

"Papa, my face looks worse than it feels," said Mama. "Please don't be upset. I'm all right and Elsie's all right."

"Elsie, did you see this happen?" he asked. I nodded.

"Are you all right?" he asked? "Wait...what's this?" He lifted my arm gently. My cotton sleeve slid back. Dark black and blue stripes climbed from my elbow to my shoulder.

Tears filled Mama's eyes. "I didn't know he did that, Elsie. I'm so sorry." She hugged me. "Can you ever forgive your father and me?"

"That no-good husband of yours!" Grandfather thundered. But when he saw the bloody towel wrapping Mama's hand, his anger drained away. "First, you need salve and a bandage, Fannie," he said softly. "And Elsie needs breakfast." He filled a bowl with steaming oatmeal, a pat of butter, a drizzle of honey, and a handful of raisins. "This was how your Mama like oatmeal when she was little," he said. He poured cold milk on top and I dug in. Mmm. Warm and sweet and delicious. A perfect taste to begin my birthday. Did anyone even remember?

I finished my first bowl while Grandfather cleaned Mama's hand. He pulled out a tiny sliver of glass, and Mama told him about the whiskey bottle.

"I don't want you worrying about Elsie and me," Mama said. "It's really, truly over this time. I'm never going back to Horace." She sounded like my ticket—one trip only; this day only. No going back. The future looked as blank as the whitewashed canvas walls. Grandfather wound a bandage around Mama's hand in silence. My mind drifted back to yesterday's fight.

"You don't know nothing about me!" Father had yelled. "How I work all day in a pit, digging in the dirt like an animal. Bosses yelling, 'Faster, faster! More track, more track!' I tell you, those blasted underground trains are gonna *kill* me! So if I need a drink after a hard day, by God I will have it!" I remembered how he sneered at Mama when he said, "Besides, Fannie, you make money now, right? Sewing here at home? Where's your money? You pay the rent this month."

"You stupid fool," Mama had screamed. "You sold my mother's sewing machine on Saturday, remember? And for what? A couple bottles of whiskey, that's what! I can't sew without my machine. How can I feed us now?"

I remembered last Saturday very well. How broken-hearted Mama had been to find her sewing machine gone. How I had scrunched on the floor near the window, my hands shaking, as they hurled bitter words at each other. Finally he left, slamming the door. She sobbed in their bedroom. I went into the kitchen. Father's whiskey bottle sat on the table. I sniffed it. Mama called it the devil. Father said it was a reward. I lifted the bottle and tilted it toward my mouth. The warm liquid turned to fire on my tongue. My eyes watered, I coughed, and spit the horrible stuff in the sink.

Then, for no reason I can remember, I tilted the bottle again. This time I swallowed. The whiskey burned down my throat, through my chest and into my stomach. I didn't spit. My hands stopped shaking.

"More oatmeal, Elsie?" Grandfather asked, startling me back to the present.

"Yes, please," I said, ducking my head, ashamed of my thoughts. Mama sipped her coffee. Her bowl of cereal was untouched. I gobbled down a second bowl.

"Grandfather and I need to talk," Mama said. "Why don't you go to the boardwalk and see the ocean? We can relax now. Your father's not here."

I walked to the beach. A group of girls held hands and jumped in the waves. Molly and me could do that, I thought. But first we'd need their black wool bathing dresses, long wool stockings, and frilly white bathing caps.

I looked out at the horizon, where the deep blue sea lined up against the light blue sky. It stretched for miles. Not one single building blocked the view. I most definitely was not in New York City anymore. No clanging trolleys. No street peddlers yelling, "Fresh fish!" Or, "Cabbages! Pickles!" No newsboys pushing papers in my face. "Extra! Extra! Read all about it!"

No, here it was just the ocean and the sky. I watched wave after wave rise in the sea, then crest, curl over and crash on the sand. As soon as one was done, another came along and did the same thing. Over and over. Dependable. Soothing.

More memories flooded back. How Mama, Father, and I came here every summer for the National Anniversary on the Fourth of July. How we'd watch the parade and fireworks and sleep in the little tent. How we'd stay two days and celebrate my birthday on the sixth with hot dogs and sour pickles, ice cream and birthday cake. How we laughed all the time.

One year life changed. Father didn't want to come to Ocean Grove anymore. He was bored, he said. That winter Grandmother died in Pennsylvania, and Grandfather stayed in their farmhouse all summer. He couldn't bear to live in the tent alone. The next summer Mama and I helped him move into his tent. We stayed for a whole week—the happiest week of my life. But Father complained of being alone in New York, and forbade us to go again. Our summer trips stopped.

My thoughts were interrupted by singing. I walked over to a large grassy area and found an army of boys marching in tan uniforms, singing "Onward, Christian Soldiers."

"Com-pa-ny, halt!" called a uniformed man. The boys stopped instantly. The smaller ones in front carried flags or drums. The rest held wooden rifles against their shoulders, the tallest boys in back. People lined the sidewalks, applauding.

Farther down the lawn I found a huge group of girls posing for a photographer. They wore spotless white dresses and hair ribbons that blew in the breeze. The littlest ones sat in front, their dresses spread on the grass. The others stood in neat rows, the tallest in back. The photographer looked into his camera. He pulled a black cloth over his head. "Hold still now," he commanded and pushed a button. Light flashed, smoke floated in the air, and he stood up. The girls immediately began talking and giggling. I wished Molly and me could be dressed so fancy and getting our picture taken. I smoothed back my frizzy hair.

A young woman sat on a bench holding a baby. "Excuse me," I said. "Is something special happening today with all the boys and girls dressed up?"

"Where have you been, Miss?" the woman asked. "*Everyone* knows that President Theodore Roosevelt is coming here tomorrow to give a speech. These are the boys and girls of the Children's Chorus, and they'll sing for the President."

"What are the uniforms?" I asked, still fiddling with my hair.

"Are you new here?" she said, frowning. "Because everyone *knows* those are copies of Roosevelt's own Rough Rider uniforms from the Spanish-American War. What happened to your arm, Miss?"

I hadn't realized my bruise was on display. I lowered my arm and growled, "Well, *everyone knows* that you get black and blue marks when you fall!"

I rushed away, surprised at my sudden anger, and stopped in front of the Great Auditorium. I'd gone to church here with my grandparents. It looked as huge as I remembered, like a mountain blocking the sky. Red, white and blue bunting hung along the walls. I imagined that annoying woman telling me why: "*Everyone knows* it's decorated for President Roosevelt."

Mama liked the President. I hurried to tell her the good news.

CHAPTER TWO

Wonderland

Girls' Choir and Rough Rider Boys' Choir lined up on Ocean Pathway

"Mama, President Roosevelt is coming to Ocean Grove tomorrow!" I said, bursting into the tent.

"Elsie, don't interrupt us."

"But it's President Roosevelt."

"I'm too busy for such foolishness."

Foolishness? Mama thought the President foolish? Alarms rang in my head.

"So, Papa, can you take care of Elsie until school starts?" she asked.

"What?" I blurted. "Where are you going, Mama?"

"I told you we can't go home, Elsie, and I meant it. I'm leaving your father. Getting a divorce." I listened in shock.

"You know Minnie from church?" Mama continued. "She said I could share her bedroom in a boarding house near Washington Square. Away from your father. As long as I can pay my share."

"But what about me? Can't I stay too?"

"No, Elsie. The rooms are tiny; only two people allowed. Minnie told me they're hiring at a shirtwaist factory on the square I never thought I'd have the courage, but I've decided to apply tomorrow."

"Tomorrow?"

"Yes. You'll live here for the summer. Maybe you could mind someone's children? You're good at that. And we'll need the money."

"But I want to work with *you*, Mama!"

"Not in a sweatshop, Elsie. Twelve-hour days. No fresh air. No sunshine. Lots of children do it, but not you. Not yet. You're better off here, in Grandfather's tent. "

"But why can't you work here?" Her no-nonsense voice was scaring me.

"Because your Father might find me." She sucked in her breath. "And hurt me."

"I think he's too stupid to find Ocean Grove on his

own," Grandfather said.

"Papa, do you know anyone who'd hire Elsie?"

"Come to think of it, I do. There's a widow lady from England who owns a boarding house on Ocean Pathway. It's called Britannia. She needs a new girl to serve breakfast and afternoon tea in her tea room."

"You mean like a fancy English tea?" Mama asked. "Have you been there?"

"Yes. I mean, no. That is..." Grandfather's face was uncommonly red. "I was there yesterday, but drinking coffee, not tea," he explained. "Mrs. Lewis—that's her name—and I were talking, and she told me her Irish serving girl had eloped."

"Why, Papa, your face is as red as a beet. Have you been flirting with a widow?"

"Of course, not, Fannie! How could you say such a thing?"

"Then let's go to tea this afternoon," Mama said. "Even if I'm not all fancied-up like the Queen of England."

"Very funny," Grandfather mumbled.

At noon, we ate peanut butter sandwiches on the porch. The warm sun lulled us into a drowsy stupor, like a pile of newborn kittens. Grandfather went inside to nap. The next thing I knew, Mama was shaking me awake. She held a hairbrush. "Time to tame your hair, Elsie. For your job interview." My stomach flipped. A job? Me? I was only thirteen. Can you hear me, Mama? I'm thirteen. Today!

At two o'clock we left. Grandfather's face was as white as his clean dress shirt.

"Papa, are you all right?" Mama asked.

"Of course, Fannie. I just never thought I'd be asking Mrs. Lewis to give my granddaughter a job."

"Don't worry. If she runs a boarding house, I'm sure she hires people all the time." Mama leaned over and whispered in Grandfather's ear. Now what? I wondered. Was there more to this plot to get me a job? My hands started to sweat. We came to the large lawn I'd seen this morning. The marching boys were gone.

"Oh, Ocean Pathway," Mama said. "It's as pretty as ever."

"And there's Britannia," Grandfather said, pointing to a long white building that sat like a ship on a sea of green grass. Flags flapped overhead, one American, the other British. The curved wraparound porch made a perfect ship's deck with railings. I half expected it to float out to sea. Grandfather marched up the steps, his lips clamped together in a grim line. My mouth felt dry and my hands wet. We were quite the condemned pair, walking the pirate's plank.

"Look at the beautiful rose garden," Mama gushed. "Nobody grows roses like the English. Isn't it lovely?" The walking dead did not answer.

Everything changed when I stepped through the front door. Roses of every color climbed the papered walls. More roses bloomed in the green carpet under my feet. A mysterious smell, like spicy cookies, floated from a beautiful crystal bowl. Inside were dried rose petals layered with cinnamon sticks and cloves. How very odd. Like Alice tumbling down the rabbit hole, I'd entered some kind of strange new wonderland.

"Welcome to Britannia," said a woman sitting at a

desk. Her yellow hair matched a bouquet of yellow roses. Behind her stretched a long wall of bookcases, filled with books. "My name is Ingeborg. May I help you? Oh, Mr. Heines, it's you. Are you all together?"

"Yes," Grandfather said.

"Go right in, there's no line. Enjoy."

A young woman seated us at a table set with pink china plates, cups and saucers. "Hello, Mr. Heines," she said.

"Hello, Kerry," Grandfather said faintly.

"Will you and your guests be having the standard cream tea or a full high tea then?" Her lilting words reminded me of the O'Briens.

"Just the cream tea, please," Grandfather said. "And ask Mrs. Lewis if I might have a cup of her good coffee instead." He stood up and whispered in the girl's ear.

"Yes, right away, Mr. Heines," said the girl. She winked at me and left. Winked! At me!

Mama smoothed a lock of hair over her swollen eye. "I don't want to frighten Mrs. Lewis off now, do I? And sit up straight, Elsie. You never get a second chance to make a good first impression."

"How can I work here, Mama?" I cried. "I've never heard of a cream tea. I don't know a high tea from a low tea from a tea in a tornado. And people are whispering, strangers are winking, and roses smell like cinnamon!"

"Whatever are you talking about?" Mama asked. "Tornadoes and winking and such? Listen, it's perfectly normal to be anxious about new things. I'm anxious about the shirtwaist factory. None of us know what lies ahead. Let's concentrate on one thing at a time. Soon we'll know what a cream tea is. I think a high tea has sandwiches."

Kerry came back, balancing a filled tray on her shoulder. She swept it down and placed one rose-painted teapot, a matching creamer of milk and bowl of sugar cubes, tiny silver tongs, plate of scones, mug of coffee, and two tiny white pots on the table. As smooth as a magician, I thought. Grandfather lifted the covers from the pots.

"This one is excellent clotted cream that Mrs. Lewis imports from Devonshire, England," he said. "Delicious on scones. And this is her homemade strawberry jam, from good old American berries. Spread them both on your scones. Dee-licious! I guarantee it." He sipped his coffee and finally smiled.

Our mouths were full of scones, cream, and jam when suddenly the kitchen door burst open and out sailed a very broad woman. The bib of her white apron billowed over the biggest bosom I'd ever seen. She reminded me of the tall ships with windblown sails I'd seen in New York harbor.

"Mr. Heines," said the woman, "I am so sorry I couldn't get out here earlier to greet you and your guests."

"How do you do, Mrs. Lewis," Grandfather said. He stood up so abruptly that his chair teetered backwards. Mama caught it before it crashed to the floor. "Mrs. Lewis," he repeated, "may I introduce my daughter, Mrs. Frances Shaw, and my granddaughter, Miss Elsbeth Shaw. They surprised me today with a visit."

"How perfectly splendid," Mrs. Lewis said. "I've heard all about you. Oh, I mean I've heard Mr. Heines speak of you. To others, that is. And to myself. A little." She looked at Grandfather helplessly and muttered, "I sound like a bleedin' idiot."

"And we've heard of you, Mrs. Lewis," Mama said. "All very properly, of course. You have a lovely English accent." She smoothed back her hair nervously, uncovering her eye.

"Oh, dear, I'm sorry," Mrs. Lewis said. "I didn't notice you were injured."

"It's...nothing," said Mama.

"Are you here on holiday?" Mrs. Lewis asked.

"No, I'm leaving tomorrow," Mama said slowly. "But my daughter will be living with Father because...." Her voice trailed away. "Anyway," she began again, "my father told me how much he enjoys your wonderful coffee." Pink roses bloomed on Mrs. Lewis's cheeks. Mama chuckled, and I loved Mrs. Lewis for making that happen.

Grandfather cleared his throat. "Um, Mrs. Lewis, we were wondering...that is, my daughter wants to ask... that is..."

"Mrs. Lewis," Mama interrupted, "when you have a minute, may we talk about a bit of business?"

"Why certainly, Mrs. Shaw. My scones are all baked, and I'm free right now. May I join you?" Grandfather pulled out the dainty bentwood chair, and Mrs. Lewis settled herself squarely in the middle of the small round seat.

Without going into detail, Mama explained the need to leave me with Grandfather while she worked in New York City. "Papa told me you're short one server. Elsie is a hard worker and learns quickly. Would you consider hiring her?"

"Hmm. My servers are usually a little older." Mrs. Lewis frowned slightly. "How old are you, Elsbeth?" she asked.

"Thirteen!" I said, a little too loudly. "I'm thirteen today!"

"Is that so," Mrs. Lewis murmured. She took a little hand bell from her apron and rang it. "We heard there was a birthday girl." Kerry came from the kitchen with a small pink layer cake lit with candles.

"Happy birthday, Elsie Sunshine," Mama said. She kissed my cheek. "You didn't think we'd forget, did you? Make a wish and blow out your candles." I made a wish all right—a very grand wish to work in this beautiful place, to keep Mama safe in New York, to have Father stop drinking, and Grandfather be happy. I blew hard. Smoke drifted into the air from thirteen blackened wicks.

"I'm honored to be part of your celebration, Mr. Heines," said Mrs. Lewis, "but I have work to do in my office. Come see me when you're finished and we'll discuss your proposal. Oh!" She covered her mouth with her hand. "I'm referring to your proposal for your granddaughter, of course. For your granddaughter to work here. That's your proposal. I really must go now." And the large backside of Mrs. Lewis, sailing on a suddenly rough sea, rocked its way out the door.

We ate our cake in silence, each lost in our own thoughts. Mama finished first. "Do you want me to go to the office with you, Papa?"

"No, Fannie. She asked for me," he said with a smile as he picked up the bill. Mama and I went to the porch and sat in wicker rockers piled with soft pillows. I fancied myself a rich guest, here for the summer, enjoying the view of the ocean.

"I hope you get this job," Mama said. "The Britannia is a beautiful place and Mrs. Lewis seems like a kind woman. I think she and Grandfather are sweet on each other." Mama giggled. "Imagine—my tall, skinny father and the adorably round Mrs. Lewis." Their names were no sooner out of Mama's mouth than the two appeared on the porch, pink-cheeked and smiling. I stood up to hear my fate.

"Why, Elsbeth, you're taller than I thought," Mrs. Lewis said. "Good. Yes, I'll hire you, but not as a server. You'll be clearing the dirty tables when customers leave, and re-setting them. Kerry and Emily are experienced; they'll be serving. Now, as to schedule. Breakfast is open to the public from seven o'clock to ten-thirty every morning. I don't serve lunch or dinner, except for full-time help. My boarders can get their hot meals in any of the fine restaurants in Ocean Grove or Asbury Park.

"The big event of our day," she continued, "is afternoon tea. It's served from two o'clock to five o'clock every day except Sunday, when we start at one o'clock for the after-church crowd. Any questions?" I had many, but where to begin?

"Good!" Grandfather exclaimed. "I told you Elsie was smart, Mrs. Lewis. Now tell Fannie about your lunches for the Camp Meeting Association this summer."

"Oh, she doesn't want to hear that, Gunther, er, Mr. Heines."

"Of course I do," Mama said.

"Well," said Mrs. Lewis, "I've been asked to serve lunches at two state conferences this summer. One is the Women's Christian Temperance Union. I'm sure you know the WCTU is trying to stop the sale of alcoholic beverages. The other group is the New Jersey Convention for Woman's Suffrage. Those ladies want the right to vote, and rightly so, say I! They're both good causes, but not everyone agrees with them."

"That's wonderful," Mama said. "And thank you for giving Elsie this job."

"You're very welcome," said Mrs. Lewis, looking me up and down. I squirmed. "Elsie, if I may call you that, I think you're about the same size as Kathleen. I'll give you her clothes. The ninny ran off so fast, she forgot them. She'll come to regret marrying that hooligan. A right Jack the Lad he was, worked part-time in a gin joint on the west side of Asbury Park. Not a dime to his name. Used Kathleen's money for their suppers. But she wouldn't hear a word against him."

"There she goes again," Grandfather said. "And what would 'Jack the Lad' mean exactly, Mrs. Lewis?"

"Oh, posh! It means he's not a serious man. He's silly and frivolous. I forget what you Americans know and don't know about the Queen's English." Mama poked my arm. I got the hint.

"Um, thank you so much for the job, Mrs. Lewis. I'll work hard, but..."

"But what?" Mrs. Lewis asked.

"Well...I've never actually been in a restaurant as fine as this and..."

"Now, don't be worrying about that," replied Mrs.

Lewis. "Kerry isn't exactly the fine restaurant type either, and she learned easily enough. My niece is coming this weekend to fill in for Kathleen, so I won't need you until Monday. Feel free to come in and observe any time."

Kerry stepped out on the porch. She looked younger in the sunshine. Fifteen, maybe? Her strawberry blonde hair shone in the sun. Her eyes were a perfect St. Patrick's Day green. I felt a twinge of jealousy, picturing my brown eyes and hair.

"Kerry, just the girl I want to see," said Mrs. Lewis. "This is Elsie Shaw. She's starting work here on Monday. She'll clear and set tables. I expect you to show her around and help train her."

"Yes, ma'm. Kathleen's not returnin' then? I was hopin' she would."

"Well, put that right out of your head. You Irish stick together, but I won't take anyone back who leaves without notice."

"Hello, Kerry," I said. Her eyes bored into mine. They flashed with pure, green hatred. I felt like I'd been slapped.

"Where are you off to now, Kerry?" Mrs. Lewis asked. "Asbury Park again?"

"A walk," Kerry said. "Don't know where yet. It's me free time."

"Go show Elsie the kitchen first," Mrs. Lewis commanded. "If that's all right with you, Mrs. Shaw? And I'll bring you Kathleen's clothes?"

Mama nodded. "Thank you, and please call me Fannie. Elsie, I'll see you at the tent." She sounded relieved. And why not? She didn't have to follow an angry green-eyed monster into a strange wonderland of cream teas and cinnamon roses.

Kerry never stopped complaining as she showed me the pantry and dining room. Seems I was just the latest in a long line of people she hated—her parents first for dying so young in Ireland; her grandparents for raising her with iron fists; and her pretty aunt who sponsored her in America, then disappeared. Poof! Just like that. Kerry was sure her aunt had run off to Paris with a rich Frenchman. Sure that she'd return and take Kerry to live with them in their mansion. Or castle. Kerry spoke well of Kathleen, the one who had brought her to Ocean Grove to work, but now even Kathleen was gone. Anger wafted off Kerry like perfume.

"Thanks for ruining my break," she hissed. "I sure don't need no spoiled baby to train. And I ain't afraid of your hoity-toity family that knows Mrs. Lewis. This ain't no easy job, you know. I should be paid for teaching you. Two cents a day."

"What?" I exclaimed. "I don't even know what I'm earning. I can't pay you."

"Yes, you can. Kathleen did it to me, and now it's my turn to get it from you. You won't last a week without my help, girlie, and you *will* pay." Kerry pushed the kitchen door open, and heat blasted my face. The warm, yeasty smell of baking bread filled the room.

I stood still, waiting to be introduced. Kerry said nothing. Neither did the stooped man sweeping the floor. Or the short white-haired woman washing the long work table in the center of the room. We all just looked at each other. The back door opened and an older girl walked in.

"Who's this?" she asked. "Is Kathleen replaced already?"

I decided to introduce myself. "I'm Elsie Shaw. Mrs. Lewis hired me to clear and set tables."

"Hah," snorted Kerry. "Emily, this girl is hired 'cause she's the granddaughter of that old coot who comes every day to drink coffee and stare at Mrs. Lewis."

That broke the ice, if ice could exist in this oven of a room. The man introduced himself as Philip and his wife as Patience. Philip told me he cooked the pancakes and eggs and bacon and sausage for breakfast and his wife made the oatmeal and toast.

"Oatmeal and toast?" Patience had a surprisingly large voice. "What about the hundreds of fancy-schmancy finger sandwiches I make for high tea, Philip? Did you forget about those?"

"No, my dear, you just interrupted me before I could say it," Philip said with a mournful sigh.

"And what about the dinners I make for Mrs. Lewis and all the staff?" Patience said. "Roasts and potatoes? Stuffed chicken?"

"Well, that's a lot of wor…" I started to say.

"And Philip and me do the dishwashing and sweeping," she interrupted.

"What about…" I began, before the improperly named Patience interrupted again.

"And we clean the stove and ice box. So there." With that, Patience dropped out of sight. Had she fallen? No one moved to help, so I raced around the table. Patience stood on the floor next to a footstool, removing her apron. She was shockingly short. The shortest adult I'd ever seen.

"I'm not no dwarf, or midget, if that's what you're thinking," said Patience. "I'm just petite. Philip, I'm going to our room to rest."

Philip shook my hand. "Welcome to Britannia's tea room, Miss. You've gotta be mad as a hatter to work here!"

CHAPTER THREE

"Our Horrible Little Parade"

*President Theodore Roosevelt
as he appeared in Ocean Grove, 1905*

I bounced down the steps of Britannia, as light as a soap bubble. Yesterday's scared little runaway was today's working girl, earning her own keep in a boarding house as beautiful as wonderland. Yes, sir, Mama was right—no dirty sweatshop for me!

Mama popped the bubble as soon as I walked in the tent. "Go pump water, Elsie. Kathleen's clothes need a good washing. Beggars can't be choosers, but we can be clean." She held a black skirt up to my waist. "You're about the same height as this girl. Good. I won't spend the whole night hemming."

We both saw the puddle spreading on the kitchen floor at the same time.

"Papa," she called, "your ice box tray overflowed."

He rushed in. "Darned ice melts too fast in this heat," he said. "I'll empty it."

"No, no," Mama said. "Elsie can do it. That's a good chore for her this summer."

I kneeled down, dragged the tray out slowly, and emptied it on the neighbor's flower garden. Grandfather kicked it back under the ice box and mopped up the puddle. Mama handed me the oak bucket. I filled it at the well, then emptied it into two pots and set them on the stove. When the water was hot, I poured it into the washtub, added flakes of soap and Kathleen's clothes.

"I'll scrub, Mama," I said. "Keep your bandage dry." I rubbed the clothes, one piece at a time, up and down the ridges of the washboard. Then I pumped more water, rinsed the clothes, wrung them out, and pinned them outside on the clothesline. By now it was time for supper. Grandfather made us cold roast chicken sandwiches.

"How about we walk over to Bradley Beach?" he asked after we'd eaten. "Just leave the dishes."

We hadn't gone very far on the boardwalk when Mama exclaimed, "Look, Papa, there's Molly." Molly? I wondered. My friend Molly was here?

"Where, Mama? Where's Molly?"

"It's not your Molly, Elsie. It's my mother's Molly. It was her name for that statue." A beautiful white stone angel sat on a tall pedestal facing the town. Her back was to the ocean.

"I don't remember it," I said. "Was it here when I was little?"

"Sure, the Angel of Victory's been here, what, thirty years, Papa?"

"Just about. It honors the soldiers who died at the Battle of Monmouth, a few miles west, in Freehold. The statue faces that direction. George Washington led the troops. Did you read about it in school, Elsie?"

"I'm not sure."

"Ever hear about the brave woman named Molly who took pitchers of water to men on the battlefield? It was blistering hot and the soldiers were suffering heat stroke. 'Water!' they'd cry. She risked her life, pumping water and taking it to them. Over and over they shouted, 'Molly, a pitcher. Over here.' As they tired it shortened to, 'Molly, pitcher!' And that became her nickname, Molly Pitcher."

"I've heard of Molly Pitcher!" I exclaimed. "Imagine—a statue of her right here in Ocean Grove."

"No," Mama said. "It's not a statue of Molly Pitcher. It's an angel, honoring soldiers who died beating the British.

My Mama just liked calling her Molly." I walked around the statue, admiring her soaring wings. She held a victory wreath in her graceful hands. I couldn't wait to tell my Molly about this Molly.

Mama yawned as daylight drained from the sky. Soon I yawned right along with her. We dragged back to the tent. Grandfather spread an old bedroll on his floor. "It's better than sleeping on pine needles," he said, "but not much. I'll get a cot for you tomorrow, Elsie. You won't sleep on the ground all summer."

It felt like only minutes later when I heard Mama say, "Time for breakfast, Elsie Sunshine." We were eating oatmeal when a familiar, angry voice shattered the quiet morning.

"Where ish she? Where's my wife? Fannie? Fannie, get out here! Right now!"

"I didn't think Horace would remember how to get here," Mama wailed. "We're trapped!" Her shoulders drooped. She shrank before my eyes.

"Outside, Mama!" I yelled. "Get outside. He won't hurt us with people watching." We burst from the tent and there was Father, bent over with his hands on his knees, gasping for air. He saw us! I grabbed Mama's good hand and pulled her toward Main Avenue.

"Stop them," Father panted. "Stop, thief!"

Crowds filled both sides of the street. I tried to push through. "We were here first, Miss," grumbled a man. "Find your own spot to see President Roosevelt."

I heard "Stop, thief!" again, and a police officer raised his nightstick out sideways. Mama slammed into it. She fell backwards, landing hard on the pavement. She buried her head in her hands and cried. The crowd fell silent. I knelt by her.

"Stop her. Stop the thief," Father yelled again. People parted as he pushed through. His dirty clothes hung like rags on a scarecrow. The police officer raised the palm of his hand and Father stopped. He coughed and spit on the ground.

"I'll start by fining you for spitting in public," said the officer. "And just what has this woman stolen?"

"What?" Father asked. His cheeks were stubbled with whiskers. His eyes darted around the crowd like a wild animal. The one person he didn't look at was Mama.

"You heard me. What has she stolen?"

"She stole my daughter. That's Elsie, my daughter. I got no one at home. I'm the man of the house. Someone should care for me."

"Sure, and what a fine-looking family man you are," said the officer, waving away Father's breath. "Stay right there and don't move." He squatted beside Mama. "What's your name, ma'm?"

Mama took her hands away from her face. Her swollen black eye and puffy lip were displayed for all to see. I heard their gasps.

"Frances Heines Shaw," she said.

"And what is your name, Miss?" the officer asked me.

"That's my daughter Elsie," Father yelled. "*My* daughter."

"You be silent!" the police officer commanded. "Are you Elsie Shaw and are these your parents?" he asked.

"Yes, sir." The weight of those two words exhausted me.

41

"Well, we've had enough of a show for these folks," said the officer. "The three of you come along to the lock-up with me. There's to be absolutely no disturbance in Ocean Grove today. President Roosevelt's parade is due any minute." He grabbed Father's arm and marched him down the street. Mama and I followed.

Hundreds of eyes judged my ragged father, beaten mother, and me. Finally we walked under a sign that read "Association Building" and disappeared down the stairs to the basement. Father was locked into a window-less room.

"He can sleep the liquor off in there," said the officer. "Now ma'm, we can keep him overnight, but no longer, unless you want to press charges."

"Press charges?" Mama repeated. "What charges?"

"I don't have all day, Mrs. Shaw. I'm needed outside. If you don't want to charge your husband with assaulting you, then he'll be released tomorrow."

"What happens to us?" Mama asked.

"If you don't press charges, we'll take you back to your hotel, or house, wherever. You'll be free, but we will demand that you remain indoors until the President leaves."

"And if I do press charges?" Mama asked.

"Then you'll stay right here. When Roosevelt leaves town, we'll come back and write down your statement. Take your pick."

"I must get back to my father," Mama said. "He's alone and worried sick, I'm sure. I press no charges." A police wagon drove us to the tent.

"Fannie. Elsie!" Grandfather exclaimed. "Thank God

you're safe!"

"Remember, now," said the officer, "all three of you are to stay inside that tent until the President leaves. If we see you anywhere else, we *will* arrest you."

I stretched out on the bedroll and heard band music coming from Main Avenue, followed by wild cheering. The President had arrived! Mama and Grandfather had their heads together. Didn't they care about missing the President? I sure did. It wasn't fair! The cheering faded away. The band music grew fainter. I wondered if the Rough Riders were singing for President Roosevelt?

"Grandfather, did I see the Rough Riders when I was little?"

"Not now," Mama said.

"No, let me answer the poor girl," Grandfather said. "Here she is, trapped inside like a criminal, while the whole town celebrates. "I'm not sure if you saw them or not, Elsie. Mr. Morgan had the uniforms made after we won the Spanish-American War. That was 1898. Roosevelt was the leader of the Rough Riders. They won great battles in Cuba that helped end the war. I'll bet he's getting a big kick out of seeing those boys."

The music stopped, and quiet settled over the town like a warm quilt. My eyes grew heavy. I imagined the President in the Great Auditorium, looking like his pictures in the newspaper—wide smile, big white teeth, fist waving in the air. I fell asleep.

I awoke to the chatter of neighbors. "Did you see the President?" asked a man.

"I sure did. And did you see him shake hands with that little Rough Rider boy? Wasn't that something?"

"I was touched by that," replied a woman. "Said the boy reminded him of himself at that age. Same thick eyeglasses. Shorter than other boys. Coughing with asthma all the time. Yet look how hardy Roosevelt is today. What an inspiration for the lad."

"Hello, sleepyhead," Mama said. "I'm glad you're awake. We're going to Britannia to speak to Mrs. Lewis."

"Again?"

"Yes, again. Your grandfather and I agree you can't live here with him. It's not safe. Your father could show up any time and snatch you away. We can't risk it."

"Please, Mama, can't I stay with you in New York?"

"It breaks my heart, but no. We're going to ask Mrs. Lewis if you can sleep at Britannia. Maybe where Kathleen slept."

"What? *Live* there?"

"Poor Elsie, so much change," Mama said. "You must be brave."

"Do we have to go right now?"

"I leave today, remember? My interview is tonight, after work hours. If I get the job, I'll start tomorrow."

No, I hadn't remembered. The horrible scene on the street had pushed Mama's leaving out of my mind. I threw my arms around her waist. "Don't leave me."

"Elsie, I have no choice. I must make money. And I'm counting on your money, too. We'll need it all to live on our own in the fall." When she said it like that, I felt like a foolish little baby. I was thirteen. Time to grow up.

The Britannia was packed with customers. Mrs. Lewis

took one look at me and handed over an apron. "God Bless the King, am I glad to see you, Elsie. We're swamped with people who came to see the President and now want tea. I could use your help clearing tables this very minute, if it's all right with your mother."

"It's fine with me," Mama said, "but first, I must beg for one minute of your time, Mrs. Lewis. It's extremely urgent." They left the dining room.

"No time to miss your Mommy now," Kerry snarled. "Empty that table! Hurry!" I slipped the apron over my head and tied it. The spotless white fabric and starched ruffles gave me courage to face a roomful of strangers.

Kerry handed me a tray. I piled it high with dirty dishes. Too high. Halfway to the kitchen, the tray tipped lower and lower, until I was sure the dishes would smash to the floor. Emily came to my rescue, grabbing the front of the tray. The two of us delivered it safely to the kitchen. "Don't put so many dishes on at once," she said.

"What are you doing here?" snapped Patience. She sliced the crusts off a pile of sandwiches in four quick chops. "You're not supposed to work until Monday."

"Nope, I started today," I said. Back in the dining room, I pulled off the dirty tablecloth and spread a fresh one. I set the table with china plates, cups and saucers, and water glasses.

"Hurry up," Kerry ordered. "People is waitin'."

"Where do I put the silverware?" I asked.

"I'll show you," said Emily-the-Kindhearted. "Fork on the left, the knife and then the spoon on the right." I put the vase with its single rose in the middle of the table and stepped back. Perfect. This job wasn't so hard after all.

My triumph lasted less than a minute as the people at three tables left at the same time. I scrambled from tables to kitchen to sideboard over and over. But no matter how fast I moved that afternoon, I was always one or two dirty tables behind.

Finally the pace slowed. Tea-time was over. I met Mama in the parlor. She gave me Kathleen's cleaned clothes. "Here's your Grandmother's hairbrush, too. Papa found it for you. Now you have clothes and a bed, and Mrs. Lewis said you may eat your meals with the help. I can't possibly thank her enough."

"It's nothing, Mrs. Shaw," said Mrs. Lewis. "I'm happy to have Elsie here." She grabbed Kerry on her way out the door. "Kerry, show Elsie to your room. She'll be living there for the summer." Kerry stomped to the staircase.

"Here are sheets for your bed, Elsie," said Mrs. Lewis. "You can make it later. Hurry back down. The train won't wait for your mother. Don't worry, Mrs. Shaw," I heard her say. "You can see the room on your next visit. It's warm on the fourth floor, but her room has a window. With an ocean view."

"A window?" I heard Mama say. "How wonderful."

We climbed the rose-carpeted stairs to the second floor. "These are the guest rooms, for customers only," Kerry said. "They get all the fancy carpeting and curtains." The next set of stairs, to the third floor, was plain painted wood. "And here's where the help stays," she said. "Everyone but Hank and Sally. They live in Asbury Park. No flowery carpet on this floor. No fancy bedding either."

"Which room is yours?" I asked.

"Oh, Kathleen and me, we liked our own little hide-away up there." She pointed to a steep set of wooden stairs. No carpet. No paint. I panted for air as we climbed. Kerry opened the door to a low-ceilinged room, thick with heat. An open window beckoned with an unbroken view of the ocean. Beds sat on either side of the window. One was bare, the other a tangle of messy bedcovers. Kerry flopped on the messy one. I threw the sheets and Kathleen's clothes on the empty bed and rushed out the door.

Kerry's voice followed me. "You've got Kathleen's clothes and Kathleen's bed, but you'll never be Kathleen."

"Thank goodness," I yelled back.

"You're a sad little mouse compared to her!" she shouted down the stairs.

Grandfather paid the penny-a-person toll as the three of us walked across the footbridge to Asbury Park. I barely breathed as we neared the train depot. Mama really was leaving. I'd never known a day without her. Passengers were boarding when we arrived. Thirteen or not, I couldn't stop the tears spilling down my cheeks. Mama hugged me tightly. She was crying too.

"I'll visit next Sunday, Elsie, I promise," she said. "I hope I get this job. I'll work hard and save every cent. I know you'll work hard too. We'll be together again when school starts in a few months. Are you all right?" Her eyes searched my face.

"Don't worry about me, Mama. I'll be fine." I am *not* a sad little mouse, I declared to myself. I will *not* have Mama worrying about me. I wiped away my tears, and stretched my mouth into a big smile.

"Don't forget, stay away from Grandfather's tent," Mama warned. "Your Father might look for you there." She hugged Grandfather. "You be careful, Papa."

"You, too, Fannie," he said. "You too."

The conductor clanged the bell. Mama climbed aboard. "I'll write to you, Elsie," she shouted. The conductor hurried her inside. The train lurched forward. Slowly the wheels turned, gaining speed. The smokestack puffed. I pulled up my skirt in a very unladylike manner and ran like a boy alongside the train. I was rewarded with a glimpse of Mama's horrified eyes glued to my bare knees. The bell clanged again, and the train chugged north. Mama was gone.

CHAPTER FOUR

A Grand View!

The famous Great Auditorium of Ocean Grove

I fell asleep my first night at Britannia as soon as my head sank into the soft feather pillow. Sometime later I heard Kerry creep into bed. And sometime after that, sunshine poured through the window. Sunshine? Where was I? Oh, no—my job! I threw on clothes, brushed my hair, and raced downstairs. Mrs. Lewis was handing out aprons.

"We start serving in a minute, Elsie," she said. "I'm afraid you missed staff breakfast. You'll have to eat afterwards."

"You should have woken me up," I grumbled to Kerry under my breath.

"What, and missed seeing you all red-faced and confused?" she said. "Never."

House guests drifted downstairs first, followed by customers from all over Ocean Grove. Tables filled, and plate after plate of bacon and eggs, pancakes, and bowls of oatmeal were eaten. The homemade muffins were a big hit. Toast was served in odd silver contraptions with little arched hoops that held the slices upright.

"It's a toast caddy," said Emily when I asked. "Mrs. Lewis brought them with her from England. See how the slices stand straight up, never touching? That keeps them nice and crisp. No other restaurant has them."

The large table by the window left. "Clear it quickly, Elsie," said Mrs. Lewis. "There's a group waiting." I lurched to the kitchen with my tray of dirty dishes. Kerry was filling her tray with four plates of bacon and eggs and two toast caddies. She hoisted the heavy tray up on her left shoulder, balancing it expertly. She made it look easy.

I set the table, and the family sat down. Kerry snuck up behind me. "You forgot the napkins," she sneered. I brought six linen napkins, apologizing profusely. Two more tables got up and left. I piled the dirty plates and cups quickly onto my tray and raced to the kitchen. I grabbed clean china from the dining room sideboard and ran around the table, slapping the plates down quickly.

Saucers, cups, napkins, water glasses, silverware. There, I could make it look easy, too!

Mrs. Lewis touched my arm. "Shhh, Elsie, you're making a racket crashing the china down. Gently, gently." Good grief—I had to be quick *and* quiet! Impossible.

Finally breakfast was over. I gobbled down blueberry muffins and a glass of milk and went outside. It was so much cooler by the water. I watched children race into the ocean, then run out screaming happily into the waiting arms of a parent. Did Mama get the job? I wondered. Was she working right now? I wished I could tell her about toast caddies. The sun got hotter, and I escaped back to Britannia. The clock in the parlor said one o'clock. Mrs. Lewis rushed in just as Kerry walked down the stairs, yawning.

"Girls," said Mrs. Lewis, "I need you in the kitchen. The town is still jammed from the President's visit, and customers are lining up an hour early for tea. Help Patience with whatever she needs. My niece is baking more scones. I'll stay out here and entertain the customers with stories of bonny old England." Kerry yawned again. "Kerry, quit yawning," Mrs. Lewis snapped. "Pretty soon we'll all be yawning, and how would that look? You should get more sleep at night."

Just before two o'clock, Patience pulled my arm. "You missed staff breakfast and lunch too," she said in her peculiar loud voice.

"I had a couple muffins earlier," I said. "I hope that was all right."

"Of course it's all right. We're not in the business of starving people around here. Eat this egg salad sandwich.

And ice tea." She waved away my thanks and climbed back on her stool. I ate quickly, then cleared, cleaned, and set tables at a furious—but quietly furious—pace. It was nearly six o'clock when the last customer left.

"Wonderful job, everyone," said Mrs. Lewis. She collected our dirty aprons. "I don't think we've ever served so many people in one afternoon. It's nearly time for staff dinner. See you at seven o'clock sharp."

I went back to the beach and sat on the sand. It was still packed with people, and no wonder. It felt a hundred degrees cooler here than the tea room. The breeze blew away the stinky smell of hard-boiled eggs clinging to my clothes. Britannia was a beehive of activity when I returned. The milk wagon, an ice truck, and the egg man all unloaded wares. Philip carried boxes inside.

"What's going on, Philip?" I asked.

"Just the usual Saturday night, Miss. You know, getting everything we need before Sunday."

"Why?"

"I thought you lived here before? Don't you remember no cars are allowed in the streets on Sunday? No driving, no parking? No bicycles? The streets are empty, except for people walking, of course."

"Empty? I don't think I remember that," I said. "Why do they do it?"

"I wonder that myself," Philip said. "Makes the town holier, I guess. But, it's kind of nice, too. You can walk without stepping in horse dung, or dodging bicycles and motor cars. Even the beach is empty. No bathing in the sea on Sunday."

At seven o'clock, I ate my first supper with the staff.

Pork chops, mashed potatoes and green beans. Applesauce dusted with cinnamon. Chocolate chip cookies. A feast compared to our simple meals at home. Emily and Anne, the laundress, ate daintily. Kerry couldn't eat fast enough. She reeked of cheap rosewater.

I sat across from Hank, the porter and gardener. He was a large quiet man, as brown as Christmas gingerbread. He downed chop after chop. His wife, Sally, sat next to him. She was one of the chambermaids. I didn't know the other one's name. Mrs. Lewis wrapped two plates of food in dishtowels and stuck them in the still-warm oven.

"You know who that's for, don't you?" Philip whispered. I shook my head. "Your Grandpa. He visits her every Saturday night. They have supper in her apartment." He leaned toward me. "And that's not all. Last week I knocked on her door and there they were, drinking sherry. I saw the bottle, plain as day. How's that for a secret in this dry town where alcohol is not allowed?"

"No whiskey?" I asked. "No saloons?"

"Nope," he answered.

"That's probably why my Father stopped coming here," I said.

"Yeah, I heard about him all right. Drunk during the President's parade."

I hung my head. Did everyone know my troubles?

Sunday morning I looked out my window at a totally empty beach. No one on the sand, no one in the ocean. It looked like Robinson Crusoe's deserted island.

Downstairs, ladies arrived for breakfast in flower-covered hats and white dresses that tucked into impossibly tiny waistbands. I knew the trick to their slim waists—whalebone corsets. Mama wore hers for special occasions. I'd pull the corset laces tighter and tighter until she could barely breathe, then knot her in. "I will never, ever wear one," I declared more than once. Mama just smiled.

The men looked uncomfortable in three-piece light woolen suits. They tugged on stiff, starched shirt collars as if loosening a noose. The children were a joy: boys in clean white shirts, thin ties, and wool knickers; girls in ruffled dresses, as frothy and white as whipped cream. A few boys and girls wore shirts or dresses striped in navy blue, like little sailors.

Sunday people not only dressed better, they ate faster, too. Men kept one eye on their pocket watches. Everyone, I learned, hurried to get good seats for the church service in the Great Auditorium.

"As you know," announced Mrs. Lewis after breakfast. "it's my Christian duty to allow you time to attend services in the Auditorium. Go and enjoy it. My niece and I will go to the Episcopal Church in Asbury Park this week. Remember, tea starts early on Sunday. One o'clock. Don't be late."

I followed Kerry and Emily down the wide open street. Not a buggy or motor car in sight. A few stragglers hurried to church.

"We're going to Asbury Park," Kerry said.

"Want to come with us?" Emily asked. "There's swell-looking boys."

"Are you going to church there?" I asked.

"No, dummy," Kerry said. "We go to have fun. There's great music. Modern music, like ragtime! Not these hymns and marches."

I was shocked they'd disobey Mrs. Lewis. But...maybe if I went with them, they'd be my friends. Organ music floated in the air. I hesitated. The girls ran off. I walked into the Auditorium.

"Only balcony seats left," said an usher, pointing to the stairs. The upstairs usher led me to the very front row, at the edge of the balcony. I walked timidly past seated people. Were they staring, or did I imagine it? I sat down and leaned over the brass railing. What a grand view! Thousands of people filled every seat below. I looked down on men's bare heads and women's fancy hats, like a bird perched high in a tree.

Suddenly the Rough Rider boys marched down the center aisle and lined up on stage. A man at the pulpit led us in prayer. "And now," he announced, "Ocean Grove's famed conductor, Mr. Tali Esen Morgan, will lead his Rough Riders Boys' Choir in the song they sang for President Roosevelt, 'Onward Christian Soldiers.'"

My heart lifted as the boys sang the very song I'd missed on Friday. As if God cared about my sadness that day, imprisoned in Grandfather's tent. As if I mattered. Everyone clapped. Mr. Morgan pulled a small boy with glasses from the front row.

"I'd like to introduce the young man President Roosevelt chose to be the Colonel of our Rough Riders," said Mr. Morgan. "His name is Theodore Whitlock, grand-nephew of Mr. and Mrs. William Lawrence who've tented in Ocean Grove since it was founded. And here's the hand that shook the President's hand!" Mr. Morgan raised the boy's right arm in the air. Everyone applauded.

The offering basket came down my row. I hadn't thought to bring money, and passed it along meekly. Next week, I'd remember. I leaned over the railing and watched the ushers march to the center aisle. They paired off in two's, and marched the baskets of money to the front. The men folk in this town, young and old, sure did like marching.

The sermon was long, and my mind wandered. Was Mama at our church today? Where would we live when summer ended? And where was Father? He could be here right now! I slouched back in my chair, trying to hide in plain sight.

Back at Britannia I ate a sandwich and put on a fresh apron. Kerry and Emily had not returned. A few minutes later they ran in, holding hands and giggling. Mrs. Lewis was waiting.

"Where have you been?" she asked, hands on her hips.

"Oh, sorry, ma'm," Kerry quipped. "We ran over to Asbury Park for one of their famous hot dogs after services."

"And how was it?" Mrs. Lewis asked.

"Delicious, ma'm."

"No, I meant the service. How was the church service?"

"The usual, ma'm. You know, singing and talking and praying. Right Emily?" Emily hesitated. Two red spots marked her cheeks like targets.

"Get your aprons on, and I'll open the doors," said Mrs. Lewis. Among the first to arrive was Theodore Whitlock and his family—parents and grandparents, a little girl with a stuffed bear, and an older Rough Rider boy.

"And how is everyone in your family today, Mrs. Lawrence?" asked Mrs. Lewis.

"Very well," she replied. "This is my nephew, Teddy. My sister's quite ill, expecting a second child, and she sent Teddy to live with us for the summer. Mr. Morgan presented him in church today as the new Colonel of the Rough Riders. I hope all this attention doesn't go to his head."

"Oh, so that was in today's service?" Mrs. Lewis said, frowning at Kerry.

"Yes, it was," said the white-haired grandmother. "Back in my day there would be no such silliness during a worship service. There was more dignity then. The boy most certainly will get a big head."

"His head looks fine to me," Mrs. Lewis said. "In fact, I saw the whole parade on Friday from my porch. What fine marching both you boys did. I even saw the President shake your hand, Teddy."

"I didn't ever want to wash that hand again," said Teddy in a squeaky, high-pitched voice. "But Aunt Gladys talked me out of it." The family laughed. Teddy had their full attention. Even the little girl's.

"Shake my Teddy's bear hand," she demanded sweetly. "He's named for your President."

"Not again, Sarah," Teddy said with a groan. "Everyone already knows your bear is named for Teddy Roosevelt, because he wouldn't shoot a bear cub on a hunting trip." He shook the bear's paw, and people at nearby tables clapped.

The quiet older boy did not speak. His hair was rusty

brown and his face a map of freckles. I liked looking at him. I liked his stillness. Very suddenly, he looked up and our eyes locked. My cheeks burned, and I turned away. Mrs. Lewis said her good-byes.

Kerry called me over to the table next to the Lawrences. "Put the teapot on the table, please," she said. "You know, it's too bad you missed seeing the President and the Rough Riders, Elsie," she said in a much louder voice. "I heard you and your parents were arrested Friday for disturbing the peace. Your father was drunk and punched your mother? They locked you up in the Association Building, right?" She hurried away. The Lawrences stared. I stood as if glued to the floor.

"Sam, stop staring this instant," said the mother. The older boy hung his head. "I'll speak to Mrs. Lewis about her staff later," she said. "Let's order tea."

I grabbed my tray and whirled around, knocking over a stack of china cups on the sideboard. They smashed to pieces on the floor. I dropped my tray, ran outdoors, and leaned over the porch railing. Now people waiting in line for tea stared at me. I hated Ocean Grove!

"Elsie, come inside," Mrs. Lewis said a few minutes later. "Philip swept up the cups."

"I'm sorry I broke them," I wailed, "but did you hear what Kerry said?"

"Yes, we all did, I think. But you know the true story of that day, and so do I. Hold your head high and get back to work. I need you. We're very busy. Don't worry about Mrs. Lawrence. I'll talk to her."

Tables began to empty. I cleared and set them, my body drooping under all the watchful eyes. Even Sam looked, but I felt no judgment when our eyes met again. It was more like puzzlement. As if he were a naturalist and I a strange bug he'd pinned in a box. A new species he was trying to identify.

Later, I overheard Mrs. Lewis. "Don't be concerned about Elsie, Mrs. Lawrence. Yes, her father was bladdered, er, drunk, and they threw him in the lock-up, but I can vouch for the girl's integrity. And I'll put a stop to Kerry's gossip."

Whatever was she talking about now? Bladdered meant drunk? Vouch for my integrity? Like Alice, I was finding this wonderland curiouser and curiouser.

CHAPTER FIVE

"Seven Lilies Dropped in the Mud"

Horses pull a steam fire engine as they race to put out a fire

Grandfather came for breakfast on Monday. "Sorry I didn't see you yesterday, Elsie. The town was too crowded, and I was plain tuckered out." He yawned. "No sign of your father. I'm sure he's gone back to New York City."

"I hope so. Mrs. Lewis thought you might come today,

and said I could serve you. She's busy baking. Would you like oatmeal? And muffins, or toast?"

"Yes, oatmeal. And toast. How did you like working?"

"It was so busy! But I know how to set a fancy table now." I decided not to tell about Kerry's gossip and the broken cups. "Guess what, Grandfather? I went to church by myself—way up in the balcony."

"Good for you, Elsie. I didn't get there myself. How was the service?"

"The best part was the Rough Riders Boy's Choir. They marched in and sang 'Onward, Christian Soldiers' just like they did for President Roosevelt. And they introduced Teddy Whitlock, a little guy who shook hands with the President. He's the new Captain, or Colonel, or something."

"Those Rough Riders are good boys, very disciplined," Grandfather said. "They'll make fine soldiers someday. I'm still sorry we missed the President..." His voice trailed off. His eyes were dull this morning. Black circles hung below them, like smudges of charcoal. Poor Grandfather.

"I'll be right back with your coffee." I blew him a kiss.

By Wednesday, life had settled into a routine, and I began to relax. Kerry tormented me less. I guess Mrs. Lewis had scolded her for blurting out my problems in front of the customers. We worked together, not like friends exactly, but at least not as enemies. She was hardly ever in our bedroom, except very late, after I'd gone to sleep.

Mrs. Lewis called a meeting of the kitchen staff after

breakfast. "With all the excitement of your American President's visit, I nearly forgot that we're to serve lunch on Friday to the Women's Christian Temperance Union! I'll need extra help making sandwiches and serving. It's a buffet at the Youth Temple. No tables to set, and easy to serve. Any volunteers?" No one raised a hand.

"Do any of you know what the WCTU is?" she asked. "Surely, you know the temperance ladies are against the sale of alcoholic drinks. They want to shut down saloons so a man can't go on payday and drink away his week's wage. Drink until he's too drunk, or broke, to buy groceries or pay rent." Philip pointed at me, and pretended to drink from a bottle. Kerry laughed.

"Laugh if you want, Kerry," said Mrs. Lewis, who hadn't seen Philip's little charade. "Maybe you don't know the WCTU also fights to keep children in school and out of sweatshops." She raised her voice. "You girls could be working your fingers to the bone in a New York sweatshop right now. All day, into the night. No school, no play, no sunshine. You wouldn't be so full of malarkey then. That means nonsense, by the way."

She sipped her tea. Was she finished? I had decided to volunteer, but didn't want to interrupt her.

"You know what I like best about the WCTU?" she continued. "It supports women's suffrage. Women's right to vote. We need to vote and make new laws that end child labor. Laws that keep children in school. And end the abuses of sweatshops. Now I'm British and answer to King Edward VII, but I'd become an American if I could vote, by God I would! Enough sermonizing. Anyone volunteer to serve lunch?"

I raised my hand. Kerry and Emily giggled. "I was hoping you would, Elsie," said Mrs. Lewis. The meeting was over.

Ingeborg waved from the parlor. "Yoo-hoo, you've got a letter," she said. I read the return address. From Mama! I ran up to my bed and tore open the envelope.

My Dear Daughter Elsie,

I miss you so much! We've never been apart since you were born. How is everything at Britannia? I hope Mrs. Lewis is as kind as I guessed her to be. How is Grandfather? Please write and tell me everything.

I got the job at the factory! I work from 7 a.m. to 8 p.m., with a short break for lunch. I'm working as a finisher—hand sewing hems and buttonholes. I make ten cents an hour. Women running sewing machines make fourteen cents. I heard some of the men on machines get more—up to twenty cents an hour! Are they really that much faster?

The foreman asked if I knew how to run a sewing machine. I said yes. Maybe I'll get promoted! I'll never, ever forgive your father for selling my machine.

Minnie has been such a good friend. She's a sales clerk at a dress shop and goes to suffrage meetings at night. She's very interested in getting the vote for women—and finding a husband!

I hope you are well, Elsie. I pray for you every night. I'll write again soon.

All my love, Mama.

Mama worked thirteen hours a day. Was that a sweatshop? Downstairs, I asked Ingeborg for a piece of stationery. She sat me at her desk with paper, pen, a bottle of ink, and a lovely rolling blotter.

Dear Mama,

I miss you too, very much. Yes, Mrs. Lewis is kind, but Kerry is not. She lied to Mrs. Lewis! Instead of going to church Sunday, she sneaked over to Asbury Park. She flirts with boys. And she's mean. She told everyone in the dining room about Father being drunk and getting locked up. I got so nervous I accidentally knocked over a stack of china cups, but it was her fault! Oops, I wasn't going to tell you that. I saw Grandfather today. He looks tired.

I went to the Great Auditorium Sunday and heard the Rough Rider Boys sing the song they sang for President Roosevelt. It made me feel good. I remember all of us going to church there years ago. Everyone was happy then.

Love, Your Own Elsie Sunshine

Ingeborg gifted me with a stamp, and I mailed the letter Thursday morning. By afternoon I was sorry I had, because I could have told Mama about the fire. We were still serving tea when the fire bell rang. Clang! Clang! Clang! Our customers rushed outside as smoke billowed over the trees.

"Bug's whiskers!" declared Mrs. Lewis. "Fire is bad in these tight quarters. One little spark can burn down a row of buildings."

"What bug? What whiskers?" I exclaimed. "Is the fire near Grandfather?"

"No it's looks further inland. 'Whiskers' are just another way of swearing without the cuss words." She opened a window. "Dark clouds rolling in. It'll rain cats and dogs in a few minutes. That'll end the fire, thank goodness. Our customers will be back soon, and not a one of them took a bumbershoot. Hurry up, girls. Make fresh pots of tea."

"Um, Mrs. Lewis, what's a bumbershoot?" I asked.

"Oh, dear, sometimes I really do forget where I am. That's an old-fashioned name for a brolly, luv. To keep dry? No, wait, you call it....umbrella, right?"

The word tumbled around my head. Bumbershoot. I liked the sound of it. So I couldn't go see the fire. Bumbershoot! And I missed the President. Bumbershoot! I'd found a new word to be my friend.

The dining room grew dark. Thunder boomed overhead. The wind picked up and appeared to blow the customers back into Britannia. Rain drops splattered the windows. I was in the kitchen filling a teapot when a dripping wet Philip burst in the back door.

"It was a tent fire," he said. "Only one tent, so that's good. Bad news, though. The firemen think it might have been deliberately set. They found a half-burned firecracker by the tent."

"That's awful," I said. "Who would do such a mean thing?"

"Nobody you know, Miss Goody-Two-Shoes," Kerry growled. "Did they arrest anyone?" she asked.

"Here's the strange thing," Philip said. "Remember

that little kid with the glasses who shook the President's hand? They think he's involved. Not accusing him exactly, but he was identified by the tent owner as being there when the fire started. The police won't do anything until tomorrow when the kid's uncle shows up."

"Ha, they wouldn't worry about that if they thought I'd done it," Kerry mumbled.

"Why not?" I asked.

"'Cause I got nobody to speak up for me," Kerry said flatly. "Nobody. My parents are dead and my grandparents can't leave Ireland. You already know my aunt ran off with her rich Frenchman. I doubt she'll come looking for little old me. So, one bit o' trouble from Kerry and it's off to the reformatory."

"Oh, that can't happen," I said. Nobody spoke. "Can it?"

Kerry's eyes flashed with anger. Anger and something else. Then I saw it. Fear crouched behind the anger, peeking out like the coward it was. Kerry grabbed a pot of hot tea in each hand. She gripped them tightly, like a two fisted boxer, and stomped out.

"That's a tough lass," said Patience. "Tough as nails."

I wasn't so sure.

Friday, after breakfast, we returned to the kitchen to make extra tea sandwiches for the WCTU. The room reeked of hard-boiled eggs. We lined up along the work table. I sliced loaves of bread, white and brown, and Emily buttered them. Mrs. Lewis cut cucumbers so thin, I could see her fingers through the slices as she arranged them on the bread. The sandwich was passed to Kerry, who cut the crusts off and passed it to Patience. She cut the sandwich into two triangles and put them on a platter.

Next came watercress. Mrs. Lewis pressed piles of the wiggly green plant between slices of buttered bread and handed them down the line. That was followed by egg salad sandwiches, then radish sandwiches. When the platters were piled high, she covered them with slightly damp linen towels. "That should keep them fresh until lunch," she said. "Now, on to the lemonade."

Philip had cut a big basketful of lemons in half. Their bright, fresh smell washed away the stink of boiled eggs. We three girls pushed the lemon halves down onto glass squeezers, twisting the fruit until the squeezer filled with juice. Then we poured it into pitchers. We twisted, squeezed and poured until our arms ached. Patience had already boiled sugar and water into syrup. She mixed the syrup with the lemon juice. Philip stabbed a block of ice with his ice pick and dropped chunks into each pitcher.

Everything was loaded into a Camp Meeting wagon and taken to the Youth Temple. We unloaded china plates, silverware, glasses, platters and pitchers. And a large vase of roses, of course.

"Well, I see lunch has arrived," said a woman in a white linen suit at the front of the room. "Perfect timing. Let us give thanks." After the prayer, Mrs. Lewis spoke.

"Good afternoon ladies, and some gentlemen, too, I'm happy to say." Her accent was as thick as clotted cream. "On behalf of my tea room at Britannia, I invite you to enjoy our authentic English tea sandwiches. There's ice-cold lemonade, and for dessert, delicious molasses cookies baked by Ocean Grove's famous Mrs. Wagner. If you need anything else, ask Miss Elsie Shaw here."

"Who, me?" I blurted. "Where are you going?"

"Yes, you, Elsie. Now shush. You volunteered, remember? Just pour the lemonade and hand out napkins. Put the cookies out when the sandwiches are done. Stay here until Philip comes for the dirty dishes. Enjoy the speeches."

After lunch the linen suit lady spoke again. "This morning we heard from temperance speakers about the evils of alcohol. Our next two speakers will talk about other causes dear to our hearts—votes for women and social justice. First, welcome Mrs. Minola Graham Sexton, President of the New Jersey Woman's Suffrage Association."

"One day women WILL vote!" said Mrs. Sexton, raising her arm in the air. Everyone clapped. What an extraordinary thing to say, I thought. She made it sound so certain. "We must not give up our cause," she continued. "Our suffrage convention meets in this same building in August, and the WCTU is invited. Our goals mesh, for as you know, political meetings in America started out in saloons, places women weren't even allowed to enter. We've been shut out of politics far too long! It's over fifty years since Susan B. Anthony and Elizabeth Cady Stanton started the fight for suffrage in 1848. That was the middle of the 19th century. That century is over. Gone. We live in 1905 now—the 20th century! Our time to vote has come! The future belongs to us!"

Everyone jumped to their feet, applauding. She continued her speech, sometimes yelling like a female

President Roosevelt. My heart pounded. I imagined putting my vote in a ballot box. I imagined standing up and giving a speech. Bumbershoot! I had no idea this meeting would be so exciting.

The next speaker was Mrs. Powell Bond, Dean of Swarthmore College. "There's a new kind of woman graduating college today," she said. "Modern women from the all-female 'Seven Sister' colleges and of course, my own Swarthmore, open to both men and women."

What? I thought, leaning forward. Colleges for women?

"When these female students graduate," continued Mrs. Bond, "they are no longer content with debutante balls and high society parties. They want to make a real difference in the world, so they've banded together as The Junior League for the Promotion of Settlement Houses. Their mission is to improve the lives of the poor. Most Junior Leaguers come from wealthy families. The ones you read about in society columns."

Of course, I thought, colleges for rich girls. No wonder I'd never heard of them.

"But these young ladies," said Mrs. Bond, "leave their mansions to live and work in the filthiest, most crowded parts of our cities. Places like the lower east side in New York City, where thousands of immigrants are crammed into cheaply made tenement buildings. Children sleep stacked together, like firewood. On a bed if they're lucky. Backyard wooden privies collect the human waste for whole buildings." Mrs. Bond sighed. "This is not a pleasant topic to speak about, but we must, for outdoor privies breed deadly diseases. A law was passed in 1901 requiring tenement owners to tear down outdoor facilities and install two water closets on every floor. Very few have done it, and disease is still rampant."

Ha! I laughed to myself. I could give my own speech about the horrors of the toilet. Mama says we're lucky to have indoor water closets, but one of the two toilets has never worked. All four families on our floor share one toilet in a tiny closet with no window and barely room to turn around. The Katz family alone has eight children, so I wait in line a lot. And the smell! The air shaft helps a little, but if big old Mr. O'Brien is in line ahead of me, I just go back home and sit with my legs crossed.

"That's where the settlement houses come in," Mrs. Bond was saying. "Progressive men build them, but it's the college women who bring the buildings to life. They teach immigrants to speak English. They teach nutrition and hygiene and child care. There are gymnasiums where they lead the children in sports and calisthenics, and public bathing rooms with tubs, hot water and plenty of soap.

"And what thanks do these 'Seven Sister' college graduates get for their hard work? A recent newspaper headline labeled them, 'Seven Lilies Dropped in the Mud.' Sounds like an insult, but it's inaccurate. Our 'lilies' from Barnard and Bryn Mawr aren't *dropped* anywhere—they *choose* to serve. Our 'lilies' from Mt. Holyoke and Radcliffe *choose* to live among the poor. The 'lilies' who graduate Smith and Vassar and Wellesley *choose* to relieve the suffering of others!"

More applause, then Mrs. Bond said in a quieter voice, "One of our graduates at Swarthmore last month, Miss Alice Paul, is a perfect example of today's idealistic young woman. Miss Paul was the honored 'Ivy Poet' of her class, and she spoke at the ceremony. I met her afterwards and learned of her plans to further her education. But first, she's chosen to live and work at the New York College Settlement House on Rivington Street in lower Manhattan."

I knew College Settlement House! It wasn't far from my home on Orchard Street. Why, I passed it on my way to school! What if I could meet Alice Paul? What if I could help immigrant children? Mrs. Bond sat down, and the lady in the now very wrinkled linen suit stood up.

"I'd like to remind you of our Temperance Service here tonight at eight o'clock," she said. "We welcome everyone, especially those seeking release from the deadly grip of alcohol. We'll have temperance pledges available to sign." She banged her gavel. "Meeting adjourned."

Philip opened the door at that very moment. We loaded up the dirty dishes and rode back to Britannia. "You're awfully quiet, Elsie," he said.

"I can't stop thinking about the wonderful speeches, Philip."

"You like that kind of thing?" he asked. "Those busybodies better not touch *my* pint of beer! I've never been drunk. Never hit my wife. Work hard every day. My evening beer is no concern of the WCTU."

Afternoon tea had started at Britannia. Gossip about the tent fire floated around the dining room. It sounded silly and petty after the uplifting speeches. A lady in a yellow hat spoke loud enough for the whole room to hear. "My brother, Louis, is a fireman," she said. "He was at the fire. He doesn't believe Teddy Whitlock started it."

A man at another table responded just as loudly, "But Teddy was the only person there. The owner of the burned tent identified him."

"I heard Mr. Morgan demoted Teddy from Colonel of the Rough Riders," said another woman. "Why would he do that if the boy were innocent? And what do we really know about this boy? Why is he here without his parents?" I spun in a circle, following this strange conversation sprouting around the room.

"Muriel, you know he's the grandnephew of the Lawrences, a good family," said the man again. "And they've taken him in for the summer."

"Well, I know why they've taken him in," said yet another woman, fanning herself. "My tent is near theirs," she confided. "Seems Teddy's family lives in a very poor part of Hartford, Connecticut. The father works long hours and the mother is ill. No one was watching the boy. Everyone knows that's how trouble starts."

A man stood up near the center of the room. "I know Mr. Morgan personally," he said, "and you won't find a finer gentleman. He only demoted Teddy for appearance's sake, until the real arsonist is found. That should be the end of that."

"But it's not," said the lady with the fan. "The trouble started when President Roosevelt picked just any boy to lead our Rough Riders. A bit too hasty, I think."

"Now what's all this malarkey?" said a familiar British voice. Mrs. Lewis swept into the room with a forced smile and flashing eyes. "I do hope you're all enjoying my raspberry tarts. I'm glad to see my customers all, um, chatting, and I wish you a very good evening in this *Christian* town we call God's Square Mile." Her words poured like water over a fire. The gossip fizzled and disappeared.

"You're distracted, Elsie," said Emily later. "Did you work hard at the conference?"

"No, it was grand. Just grand. The speakers were all women. They talked about women going to college! And helping immigrants. And voting! I want to be like them."

"College? Are you crazy?" she said. "There's no college for the likes of us."

CHAPTER SIX

All in a Day's Pay

*The fiery and famous
Temperance speaker, Carrie Nation*

Itook a walk later, at sunset. The golden sky behind the
Great Auditorium glowed like the light of a thousand
candles, held in a thousand hands. Over the ocean, the

sky was baby blue, streaked with pink clouds. Pastel east; golden west—my favorite time of day. Who wanted to go to a temperance meeting when the sky looked like this?

I walked slowly, watching couples, families, and friends stroll by. I missed Molly. And Mama, so much. What was she doing right now? Still working? Eating dinner? Was Minnie with her? The sky slowly faded to gray. I turned back, and found myself at the Youth Temple, reading a sign. "Temperance Meeting Tonight. All Are Welcome." I peeked in the door.

"And now for our final speaker, please welcome a gentleman who prefers to go by the name of John Smith," said a woman. "This fine man will bear witness to the power of the temperance pledge, a document that lifted him from the gutter back into the arms of his family." The words pulled me in, and I slipped into the back row.

"Good evening," said Mr. Smith. "I'm not much of a public speaker, but I was asked to share my story in hopes it might inspire some other poor soul. It was one year ago that I heard the famous Carrie Nation speak right outside this building, over at Beersheba Well. She was a fierce-looking lady, at least six feet tall, dressed all in black mourning clothes. She held a Bible in one hand and her famous hatchet—the one she used to smash bottles in a Kansas bar—in the other. That was the bar that sold her husband drink after drink, year after year. He lost his job, then his health. His family suffered hunger, shame, and finally, sorrow, when he died of alcoholism. Carrie Nation described his painful death in great detail.

"Her speech scared me to death. No, it scared me to life! I signed the pledge she held in her hand that day.

The good people of Ocean Grove prayed for my success. My family and I are here today to thank you."

The man's wife and three children stood up beside him. I could hardly breathe. My eyes blurred with tears. Could Father do this? The audience stood and applauded. I ran out the door, fighting tears. Someone touched my shoulder.

"I'm sorry, Miss," said a girl. Her dark hair was piled neatly on her head. "May I help you?" she asked.

"No, thank you. It's just my father...he..." I could say no more.

The girl wrapped her arms around me. "Would your father like to sign the pledge? Is he here?"

"No, he's not," I said, sniffling, "but I'd give anything if he'd stop drinking and we could live together again." I pulled out a handkerchief and blew my nose.

"Let's just watch from the door, then," she said. "Look! There's a man going forward now." A disheveled man, bent as a broken stick, shuffled up the aisle. Mr. Smith shook his hand and handed him a pen. The man's hand was so shaky that Mr. Smith guided the pen into the ink bottle. The man scratched his name on the pledge and slowly straightened up.

"Ladies and gentlemen," said Mr. Smith, "we all know a man's signature on a contract is a sacred thing. By signing the pledge, this man is promising before witnesses that he will not drink alcohol ever again. Let me read the last few lines of the pledge.

'Believing it to be better for all, and the better example, I, the undersigned, solemnly promise, by the Help of God, to abstain from the use of all intoxicating drinks as a beverage.'" Everyone clapped. The woman leader stood up.

"What a moving testimony!" she exclaimed. "Our prayers will be with both gentlemen. I'd like to remind the audience that the temperance pledge is for everyone, not just the drunkard. Two men may toast the New Year with champagne. One will go on with his life as before. The other, however, will crave alcohol again and again in any form—whiskey, gin, beer, wine. His life will spiral downward, until he and his bottle hit the bottom. No one knows if alcohol is his or her weakness until it is too late. It is better to never start, but to sign a pledge and promise a life of temperance."

"My name is Amelia Shirm," said the girl. "Do you live in Ocean Grove?"

"I'm Elsie Shaw. My grandfather has a tent, but I don't... that is, I live at the Britannia. I work in the tea room."

"I've been there," Amelia said. "It's so pretty. Um, my mother teaches a Bible class right here every morning at nine o'clock. Want to come? You'd be in my class."

"Thank you, Amelia, but I work at the tea room until ten-thirty every morning."

"Can I do anything for you?" she asked.

"May I have a temperance pledge? For my Father."

"Certainly." Amelia slipped inside and came out with two pledges.

"It's better if a man signs a pledge in a public way," she said. "Having witnesses strengthens his promise. But give him one and get him thinking about it. Here's an extra one. It's a hard commitment to make, Elsie, and may take more than one attempt."

"Thank you so much," I said. "It's nice meeting you. I have to get back to Britannia now." I felt strangely uncomfortable, and remembered how Mama didn't want to answer questions, or accept charity. I was beginning to understand.

Saturday morning brought a surprise—my first payday! I hadn't worked enough last Saturday to get one. Cooks, servers, chambermaids, laundress, porter, and receptionist lined up to receive a sealed envelope from Mrs. Lewis. Each person immediately pocketed his or her envelope. Why didn't they tear them open and count the money? I sure wanted to. For three hours the mystery envelope hid in my apron pocket, its slight weight banging gently against my leg.

As soon as breakfast was over, I raced upstairs, tore open the envelope and dumped the money on my bed: one dollar bill, four quarters, one dime, and one nickel. Two dollars and fifteen cents! I'd never held so much money in my life. Kerry walked in. "How much did ya get?" she asked.

"Why do you want to know?"

"I want me share for trainin' ya," she said.

"You didn't train me. I taught myself."

"That ain't true, you little mouse! You didn't know where anything was. You owe me two cents a day. Fourteen cents."

"You're crazy," I yelled. But Kerry had already swooped over and grabbed the nickel and dime.

"Fifteen cents!" she hollered joyfully. "One extra penny

for giving me a hard time." The thief ran downstairs. I was left with two dollars even. I scooped it back into the envelope. I needed a hiding place. I put the pay envelope and the temperance pledges in my apron pocket and went to visit Grandfather. He sat on his porch, reading the newspaper.

"Hello, Grandfather."

"Elsie, what a surprise! It's good to see you. But you're not supposed to be here, are you?" His eyes darted left and right, as if Father were lurking behind every tree. "Elsie, what would you think about calling me Grandpa? Or even Gramps? Grandfather sounds so formal."

"Sure! Grandpa it is—unless I forget. Guess what? I got paid today!"

"You did? How much did you make?"

"Well, um..." I didn't know what to say about the fifteen cents, so I just dumped the money on his table.

"Will you look at that?" he said. "A dollar bill and four quarters. Two dollars, Elsie! I'm so proud of you. How about a hug?" Instead, I stomped my foot.

"I'm too mad to hug," I shouted. "That thief Kerry stole fifteen cents. Payment for training me, she said. It's not fair, Grandfath...Grandpa!"

"What? That nice server took your money?"

"Yes. And she's *not* nice. She said that Kathleen, the girl who eloped, took money from her and now it's her turn to take it from me. Every week."

"That's outrageous," he said. "I'll speak to Mrs. Lewis about this."

"Please don't, Grandpa. I have to take care of it. Kerry's not getting one cent more, I promise. Can I hide my pay in your tent?"

"Of course you can. I won't tell Mrs. Lewis unless Kerry steals again. Hey, let's figure out how much money you made per hour."

Grandpa got pencil and paper and had me add up my hours. Three hours in the morning, and three hours in the afternoon. Six hours a day times seven days a week. That came to forty-two hours. "Oops," I said. "I forgot Sunday. Afternoon tea is an hour longer, so that's forty-three hours. And two dollars fifteen cents divided by forty-three hours is...five cents an hour!"

"That's good, Elsie, especially since Mrs. Lewis gives you free food and lodging. Very generous."

"Can we find a hiding place now?" I asked.

"Sure, I know just the place," he said. He kneeled beside his bed and pulled out a pretty painted box. "This was your Grandmother's. I bring it every summer—keeps her close to me. The painted flowers are called rosemaling in Norway. Go ahead, open it." I lifted the lid. Inside was a bundle of letters tied with a ribbon. "Our old love letters," said Grandpa with a sigh. "I'll take those."

"It sure is pretty," I said. "Can I keep my money here?"

"Of course, honey. But don't put it all in. I'm sure your mother wants you to buy a little treat for yourself."

"No, we'll need all our money in the fall, Grandpa. I'm saving every cent." I showed him the temperance pledges for Father.

"Elsie, don't put too much hope in those pieces of paper. But, it's a start." I put everything in the box and pushed it under the bed.

"Thank you, Grandpa." I kissed him good-bye and went

for a stroll through the tent colony. Tent families live on their porches and I like walking by, watching them eat, read, mend clothes, play with children, or just sit and fan themselves. A bicycle leaned against a front yard fence. A boy knelt down, fixing a tire. He stood up suddenly. It was Sam Lawrence!

"Oh," he exclaimed. "Hello, Miss. I didn't hear you."

"Hello," I said. "Are you fixing your bicycle?" What a dumb thing to say, I groaned to myself.

"Yes," he mumbled. Then nothing. I kept walking.

"Miss," he called. "Are you the girl who works at Britannia?"

"Yes," I said, turning.

"Is your name Elsie?"

"It's Elsbeth, but everyone calls me Elsie. And you're Sam?"

"Yes. You know, that serving girl was stinky talking about you in front of everyone at Britannia. Very rude."

I laughed and said, "Stinky Kerry. I like it."

"Do you live in a tent?" he asked.

"No, but my grandfather does."

"Where are you staying?"

"At the Britannia, on the top floor."

"Are your parents there too?"

"No." I backed away. Sam asked too many questions. I didn't ask if his cousin started the fire, did I? "Nice meeting you, Sam. I have to go now. Good-bye."

"Good-bye."

I didn't want to talk about the fire, but it seemed everyone else at tea that afternoon did. Once again wagging tongues gossiped: had Teddy set the fire? Was he a danger to the community? Should Mr. Morgan have demoted him? I wanted to scream, "Shut up, everybody!" but of course that would never do at a proper English tea.

"What are you all upset about?" Kerry asked with a smirk. "Still mad about paying me?"

I glared at her. The gossip, Kerry's smirking, Sam's questions, it all made me want to...want to...I suddenly realized what I wanted was a sip of Mrs. Lewis's sherry. Philip told me she had some. Very casually, I left the dining room. Ingeborg was in the parlor, talking with guests. Mrs. Lewis was baking scones. I slipped into her office and opened the door to her private apartment. Two bottles were in a cabinet. One was half empty. It smelled so much better than Father's whiskey. I swallowed a sip. It tasted better too. Sweeter. Four—maybe five—sips later I eased back into the dining room.

"Girl, where have you been?" Kerry asked. "And what are you smiling about?"

"Nothing," I replied.

She leaned in and sniffed my breath. "You've been drinking!" she exclaimed. "Where did ya get it?" I stayed quiet. "Aha—I know!" she said. "Philip told you Mrs. Lewis's little secret, didn't he? Her sherry?" I was beginning to panic, but said nothing.

"Well, now, ain't this a kick?" snarled Kerry. "Little Miss-Butter-Won't-Melt-In-My-Mouth likes to tip the bottle. Very good to know. I should tell Mrs. Lewis."

"Please, Kerry, please don't tell her."

"Maybe I won't," she said, "or maybe I will."

I was clearing tables next morning after a fitful night's sleep when Grandpa walked in—with Mama! I raced into her arms. Mrs. Lewis walked straight toward me. Oh, no, I thought, Kerry had told her! Now she was going to tell Mama!

"I've decided your mother and grandfather are going to have a free breakfast, Elsie," she said, "and you are going to serve it. Think you can do that?"

"Oh, yes, Mrs. Lewis," I said, my whole body exhaling with relief. "I'm sure."

"Good. Come along, Mrs. Shaw. It's good to see you again. And Mr. Heines."

I took their orders to the kitchen, and brought Mama her full teapot and Grandpa his coffee. I balanced her order of pancakes and maple syrup, and his bacon and eggs and toast on my tray and served them perfectly. I explained the toast caddy to Mama. I felt so proud and happy, I nearly curtsied!

"Nice job," said Kerry the thief, walking by. "No, I mean it. You're lucky to have a Mum. Don't mess it up." My mouth fell open. A compliment from Kerry? After breakfast, Mama and I ran up to my room.

"What a view!" Mama exclaimed, looking out my window at the ocean. She stopped to catch her breath, then asked, "Can you hear the waves at night?" I nodded. "You know, Minnie and I sleep in one of the cheapest rooms in the back of the boarding house," she said. "There's no window. It doesn't matter because we're never there except to sleep, but I'm so glad you're not jammed in with us. I miss you terribly, Elsie, but it warms my heart to see you in this lovely place."

Back at the tent, Mama handed me a sack of my own clothes. "I picked these up at our apartment this week," she said. "There's not much left. Your father wasn't even there." I dragged the rosemaling box from under the bed.

"Mama's treasure box!" my Mama exclaimed. "I haven't seen it in ages."

"Grandpa said I could keep my pay in it. See?" I took the dollar bill and four quarters from the envelope.

"Two dollars!" Mama said, smiling. "That's terrific."

"Fannie," Grandpa said, "I wondered if I might give the box to Elsie as a reminder of her grandmother? Or do you want it?"

"Papa, that's so thoughtful. It'll be our belated birthday gift to you, Elsie."

"Thank you both," I said softly. "I'll keep it always. Except for now, when I'm leaving it here. Right, Grandpa?"

"Sure. It's safe here."

"Why, is something wrong?" Mama asked.

I hesitated. Grandpa said nothing.

"Good," said Mama, the firm believer that no news is good news. "Let me tell you what happened on my first pay day. I wrote that I earned seven dollars and fifty cents, but that's not the whole story. I didn't tell you the foreman robbed me."

"That's terrible!" Grandpa exclaimed. "Did you call the police?"

"It wasn't like that, Papa. Right after he paid me for the seventy-five hours I worked, he told me about the company's rental system. Told me I had to pay a penny an hour to rent the chair I sat on to sew. Seventy-five cents! Can you believe that? Then he charged me two cents for every needle I used. Six more cents.

"I can still hear his gravelly voice: 'That's eighty-four cents you owe me. Now!'

"'What?' I yelled back. 'I have to give you eighty-four cents?'

"'Only if you want to keep your job,' he growled. 'Maybe move up, like to a sewing machine?'

"You see, Papa, he's counting on me not to make trouble. He knew I wanted to run the machine and make more money. Still, I had to fight back—it just wasn't right. 'What about my lunch?' I asked him.

"'What about it?' he replied.

"'I don't eat lunch sitting in that chair,' I said. 'I go outside. That's three cents I shouldn't have to pay.'

"'You're a cheeky thing, now, aren't you?' he snarled. 'Keep your bloody three cents, and give me eighty-one cents. I've a good mind to fire you this minute.'

"My pay was reduced to six dollars and sixty-nine cents," said Mama, sighing. "Then Mrs. Lowell asked for the rent. My half of the room costs two dollars and twenty-five cents a week. That includes breakfast and dinner so it's not too bad. Lunch too, since I take extra toast or rolls at breakfast to eat for lunch. I opened a savings account at J. P. Morgan's Bank with three dollars and twenty-five cents. I still had enough for my train ticket." I marveled at the new-found confidence in Mama's voice.

"Mama, want to see my temperance pledges?" I pulled them from the box. "They're for Father to sign and promise never to drink again. Then we can all live together. It might take two tries, so I have two pledges."

Mama wrapped me in a hug as tight as any corset. "Sweet Elsie Sunshine, we can only hope and pray," she said. "Hope and pray."

CHAPTER SEVEN

900 Marching Children

The Royal Court of Queen Mab III at Children's Festival

Mama's visit lifted my spirits that whole week. On Friday, Grandpa invited me to join him and Mrs. Lewis at the Children's Festival at seven o'clock. Right after dinner, I dressed in my best shirtwaist and fussed with my hair. "Hey," Kerry said, "you got a sweetheart? You're really brushing that hair."

"Of course not," I protested, blushing as if my underwear was showing. "I'm going to the Children's Festival."

"Yeah, I heard about that," said Kerry. "Lots of wee ones singing and dancing. Ain't for me. Me and Emily's goin' to Asbury Park. We met two new fellas. Nice boys. They work a shell game on the boardwalk. Have you seen it? There's three seashells, one with a quarter under it. They mix up the shells, sliding them all around. Customers pay a nickel and try to guess which shell has the quarter. If they guess right, they keep the quarter. But it's hard to win, because those boys know a trick or two—like distracting people's eyes, just for a second. Anyway, the boys treated us to ice cold Coca-colas, and we rewarded them with kisses! You should come."

"Heavens, no," I said. "I don't want to kiss a stranger."

"All right," she said, "but ya gotta kiss a fella sooner or later. The way you're working that hair, I'd say sooner!" She laughed and ran down the stairs.

The Great Auditorium was surrounded by children when we arrived. Inside, the stage had transformed into a dazzling, magical fairyland. Great loops of white electric lights hung overhead, mixed in with Chinese paper lanterns of every color. Garlands of flowers decorated the stage. A small pavilion, framed with red velvet curtains, trimmed with gold fringe, sat in the middle. Inside it was a throne. We found seats just as Tali Esen Morgan walked on stage.

"Good evening, ladies and gentlemen," he said. "Welcome to our famous Children's Festival. We've planned a wonderful concert. Besides the fine singing of our Rough Rider Boys' Choir and equally talented Girls' Choir, there will be many specialty acts: soloists, quartets, dancers, and instrumentalists. First, Mr. Fitzgerald will lead us in prayer." We bowed our heads. After the prayer, Mr. Morgan shouted, "And now I present the 900-voice Children's Choir of Ocean Grove!"

He raised his baton, trumpets blared, and children marched in through every door. I had no idea there were so many doors! At least twenty rows of children streamed in through twenty doors, all at the same time. They marched toward the center aisle, paired up in twos, and marched up onto the stage.

"And now the older children of this year's festival," Mr. Morgan said, "Queen Mab III and her Royal Court, complete with prince, courtiers and ladies-in-waiting." A single row of older girls in flowing pastel gowns entered from the back and glided down the long aisle, their arms overflowing with roses. "A good many of those flowers came from my garden," whispered Mrs. Lewis. Some of the boys wore silk stockings, satin trousers and shirts, and powdered wigs. Others were dressed in bright military uniforms.

The queen swept by in a regal white gown, purple robe edged with fur, and a golden crown. Her prince wore a red military jacket, black pants, and a hat topped with a plume of white feathers. The queen sat on her throne in the pavilion and the court arranged itself around her. They looked like European royalty. I'd never seen anything so beautiful. How I wished Mama could see it. She would love the ball gowns.

The show began with the combined choirs singing four or five lively songs. Next came girls in silk kimonos, mincing across the stage in tiny steps as they twirled paper parasols and sang a Chinese song. Boys dressed like

Indians did a rain dance to the beat of drums. A quartet of older girls played coronets. Four boys sang in barbershop harmony. The choirs took turns singing—hymns, folk tunes, patriotic ballads. I searched for Sam, but couldn't find him. Teddy was easy to spot in the front row.

When it was over, the 900 children marched expertly back outside to wild applause. Parents rushed to claim their young performers.

"Look," said Grandpa. "They're serving the children ice cream at that table. Wish I was young enough to get in line. Why don't you go get some, Elsie?"

"All right." I got in line. When it was my turn, a woman with a large scoop asked, "What flavor would you like?"

"Strawberry, please," I answered.

A second woman came over. "Did you sing tonight, Miss?" she asked. "You're not in a white dress like the others."

"What?" My face suddenly felt hot.

"Did you sing? The ice cream is only for performers." Girls behind me in line giggled.

"Oh, oh, oh." I turned to escape and ran straight into the billowy bosom of Mrs. Lewis, who had walked up behind me. I hardly knew where to set my eyes.

"I'm sorry, ladies," Mrs. Lewis said. "My friend sent his granddaughter over for ice cream. Is it not for all children?"

"No, Ma'm. Just the performers."

"Well, this is Elsie Shaw. I've heard her humming some of the songs sung tonight, and she has a lovely voice. She would be in the choir except she's too busy earning money for her family to go to the rehearsals. She works for me at the Britannia. I'll gladly donate toward expenses if you'll give her a spot of ice cream."

"No need of that," said the lady with the scoop. "You're the Mrs. Lewis who gives those lovely English teas, aren't you?"

"Yes. Thank you for the compliment."

"We don't mean to slight anyone," said the ice cream lady, "but it's impossible to treat every child in town. You understand, I'm sure." She plopped the ball of pink ice cream on a sugar cone. "Here, Elsie. Keep up the good work. You've made a favorable impression on Mrs. Lewis."

I slunk away with the ice cream I hadn't earned and took a lick. It sat on my tongue, cold and tasteless. That's the exact moment I saw Sam in a group of Rough Riders. And he saw me—with the cone. Did I imagine it, or did he frown? When, oh when, was I to learn the things that "everyone knows" in this town?

I got a letter from Mama on Saturday saying she was sick and couldn't visit tomorrow. A sadness slipped over me that even my second pay envelope couldn't shake. Mother Nature matched my mood with windy, rainy weather. Hardly anyone came to breakfast or tea. Even Mrs. Lewis was cross and snappish.

I was reading in our room when Kerry stormed in. Rain drummed on the roof and lashed against the window. "Where's your pay?" she demanded. The envelope lay, squashed and wrinkled, in my left shoe.

"It's gone," I replied.

"Give it to me," she yelled, grabbing my apron. The pocket was empty.

"You didn't teach me anything this week," I yelled back. "I'm not giving you one more cent." Kerry tore my bed apart. She looked under the mattress. She searched my clothes, throwing them on the floor.

"So I guess I'll tell Mrs. Lewis about you drinking her sherry," she said slyly.

I'd been thinking about her threat and had an answer ready. "Then I'll tell her you stole fifteen cents from me last week."

"Ha—I'll deny it," Kerry said. "You've got no proof. It'll be your word against mine."

Oh-oh, now what? I racked my brain for an answer. What had Kerry said about having no one to stick up for her? But I did—Grandpa!

"I told Grandpa about you taking my money, and he was furious. He'll tell Mrs. Lewis it's true." Kerry stomped out of the room and down the stairs. Good riddance.

The rain slowed to misty drizzle, and I ran to Grandpa's tent. The dingy canvas walls matched the gray sky. I unbuttoned my shoe and pulled out my pay envelope. "Look, Grandpa, two dollar bills this week! And coins, too. Oh, and a note from Mrs. Lewis.

Dear Elsie,

I forgot to pay you last week for working the WCTU luncheon. Two hours in the kitchen and two hours in the Youth Temple.

Sincerely,

Mrs. Lewis

"Wow, Grandfather, there's twenty cents extra for the luncheon, plus the fifteen cents Kerry didn't steal. Two dollars and thirty-five cents!" I put it all in my box.

"Here's a dime," Grandpa said, "just for fun. Buy penny candy, or whatever."

"Bumbershoot, Grandpa!"

"What's that?"

"Mrs. Lewis said it's an old-fashioned word for umbrella. I like the sound of it. It makes me happy. So... bumbershoot! And thank you!"

The rain lifted late Monday morning, and people smiled as they strolled in for tea. Even the gossip was happier. The police had caught a boy in Thompson Park, Billy Lynch, with a firecracker. The boy confessed to burning the tent.

"I knew all along it couldn't be the Lawrence's grand-nephew," wagged one tongue. "Such a good family."

"I agree," said another. "Teddy Whitlock is a fine boy, hand-picked by President Roosevelt to lead our Rough Riders." How the tide turns, I thought. At least Teddy was innocent. Sam would be happy about that.

I went to tell Grandpa the news, but he was napping. I wandered over to the Lawrence tent. Swarms of neighbors milled about, congratulating Teddy. Sarah clung to his hand. Sam stood alone near the fence, watching.

"Hi, Sam," I said. "I heard they caught the boy who started the fire."

"Oh, you again," he said. "Hi. Yeah, it's good news for

a change. I'm not surprised Billy did it. He was bad news, a real bully. Teddy saw him light the firecracker, so Billy threatened to set fire to our tent if Teddy squealed to the police. That's how Teddy got blamed. But Billy's going to reform school, and Mr. Morgan made Teddy Colonel of the Rough Riders again. Things are back to normal. I *hated* all that stinky gossip!"

"I hated it, too," I said. "You wouldn't believe all the gossip at the tea room."

Sam scowled. Oops, he didn't want to hear that. "I'm sorry, Sam. I'm always saying the wrong thing. I don't know why."

"Oh, it's all right," he muttered. "I feel that way too, sometimes. Hey, what were you doing eating ice cream the other night? Didn't you know it's just for the choirs?"

"No," I snapped. "How was I to know? My Grandpa told me to stand in line. Then the woman said I couldn't have ice cream, and Mrs. Lewis came out of nowhere and said I was a working girl with no time for rehearsals. They gave me ice cream, all right. Strawberry, with an extra helping of pity."

"Hey, that's too bad," Sam said. "I didn't mean to upset you. Between the police arresting your father on Main Avenue and now the ice cream event, you must feel pretty beat up. Can I....."

"Samuel," interrupted a voice. It was his mother. "Who are you talking to?" She shaded her eyes and saw me. "Come here, Sam. And good-bye to you, Miss."

Grandpa was awake when I returned. "Did you hear the latest about the tent fire?" I asked him.

"Can't hardly hear anything else. How are you, Elsie?"

"I'm all right, I guess. I did lots of reading over the weekend. I love the big bookcase at Britannia. Mama wrote that she didn't feel well. That's why she didn't visit. Did you hear from her?"

"Same news as you. She's working too hard. I hope she slept all day yesterday. Nothing like a rainy day for sleeping. That's what I did. Cussed rheumatism!"

I pondered Sam's words as I walked to Britannia. What was he going to ask me before his mother interrupted with those four hard, bitten-off words: "Good-bye to you, Miss." They weighed on my heart all week. The sameness of my days—eating, working, sleeping, eating, working, sleeping—was turning into a monotonous bore.

"Blimey, girl, go to the beach," said Mrs. Lewis. "I'm tired of seeing your nose buried in a book. Are you trying to read the whole bookcase in one summer? Go out and meet people. Find friends." As if it was that easy.

Thursday brought another letter from Mama. She sounded discouraged, too. I read two paragraphs over and over:

The owner of the shirtwaist factory treats us like thieves. We're locked into this building all day. It's unlocked two times, once for lunch and again at quitting time. Whenever I leave, I'm searched by the foreman. He rummages in my bag and pats my pockets and hat. Says the owner is afraid we're stealing needles or thread or whatever.

Five of us have started working an extra hour at night to earn more money, and we're locked back in after the others leave. We can't get out until the night

watchman makes his rounds and unlocks the door.
He searches me a little too carefully. I can smell the
liquor on him, and hate the way he touches me.

The Woman's Suffrage Conference began on Friday. Again, I served lunch and heard speeches. The leader was the same person I'd heard at the WCTU Conference, Mrs. Sexton. She asked why educated women who worked as teachers, nurses, and business owners were denied the right to vote?

Another speaker said women needed the vote to pass laws against sweatshops and child labor. Too many children worked long hours in factories instead of going to school because their desperate families needed every penny to survive.

"Ladies and gentlemen," said the last speaker, "we've been working for suffrage for a long, long time, close to fifty years. We must find a way to bring this important issue back into the national dialogue. Here's a poem published in the WCTU's "Crusader" magazine, way back in 1887. It's titled 'Just Before Election' and is said to have been written by a little girl:

'I'm going to be a woman,
and vote as well as you.
I'll learn while I am growing,
what voters ought to do.'

"That was written nearly twenty years ago. It's heartbreaking that this child is most likely a wife now, with children of her own. And she still can't vote!" She read the poem again. "Remember these words," she commanded, "and make them come true!"

I jumped to my feet with the audience, all of us inspired and filled with desire to make the world a better place. But what could I do? The answer came quickly—I could volunteer at the College Settlement House! I knew right where it was. And I knew someone who was there—the college graduate I'd heard about at the first conference, Alice Paul! I wrote that very night.

Dear Miss Paul,

My name is Elsbeth Shaw, but everyone calls me Elsie. I'm thirteen years old. I heard about you at a WCTU meeting. A woman from your college told us you read a poem at graduation. She said you're working with poor immigrants at the New York College Settlement House. I would like to help you. Mama says I'm good with children. Could you use my help?

I lived on Orchard Street, around the corner from your settlement house. Right now I'm working at a boarding house in Ocean Grove, N.J. and my Mama works at a shirtwaist factory in New York City. But in the fall we'll live together again in the city, and I can help care for immigrant children after school. We can't live with my father anymore because he drinks too much and fights.

Sincerely,
Elsie Shaw

I was still setting tables after tea the next day, when a friend of Mrs. Lewis peeked into Britannia. "Maude," she called, "did you hear the latest about the Lawrences?"

"Beatrix, you know I don't approve of idle gossip," said Mrs. Lewis.

"But this is different. It's just awful. It could have been worse, of course, a lot worse, but..."

"Saints alive, Bea, spit it out. What news?"

"That cute little Sarah Lawrence fell into Wesley Lake!"

"Oh, no! Tell me she didn't drown."

"Yes, er, I mean, no. Yes, I can tell you that."

"By all the crowns of England, what are you telling me, woman?"

"Yes, Maude, I can tell you that no, Sarah did not drown."

"Saints be praised," Mrs. Lewis said, blowing out her cheeks.

"That's not all," Beatrix said. "Her cousin, that little scrawny Teddy fellow, jumped in and saved her."

"Blimey, what an eventful summer that boy is having!" exclaimed Mrs. Lewis.

"But wait, there's more. Sarah's older brother, the quiet one, what's his name?"

"Sam," I said, rushing over. "His name is Sam. Is he all right?"

"Not completely. He broke his leg running to save Sarah. A bad break. His jagged bone cut right through the skin. Stuck straight up in the air. Blood everywhere. Teddy fainted dead away at the sight. After he had already saved Sarah, of course."

I felt like fainting myself. Poor Sam. How awful! Sleep that night was plagued with nightmares of drowning girls and broken bones. Sometime deep in the night, Kerry crept into bed. I thought I heard faint crying, or was that a dream too?

Grandpa came to Britannia in the morning. He drank coffee and watched the front door, hoping to see Mama. Kerry was very quiet. A purple bruise circled her neck, but she said nothing. Just as breakfast ended, Mama walked in!

"You're too thin," Grandpa chided as he hugged her. "And too pale"

"I'm fine, Papa, just a little tired," Mama said and smiled. "Nothing a good walk on the boardwalk won't cure. After church, of course."

I went upstairs to change my blouse. Kerry was in the room.

"What happened to your neck?" I asked her.

"Nothing you need to know about," she snapped.

"Did one of those 'good boys' at the shell game do that?"

"I sure didn't choke meself."

"Why'd he do it?" I asked.

"'Cause he wanted me to do things I didn't want to do, you stupid girl! I don't want to end up like Kathleen, alone, with a wee bairn on the way. She wrote me. Her boyfriend didn'a marry her like he promised. Just up and left. She's cleanin' rooms in a cheap hotel. Doesn't make much. Who knows what she'll do when the bairn is born." Tears ran down Kerry's cheeks. I started to hug her, but she pushed away.

"Come to church with me, Kerry. Me and my mother. Remember her black eye and swollen lip when we got here? We know about troubles. You'll feel better going to church, I just know you will."

Kerry shook her head and sat down on her bed.

"You *can't* go back to Asbury Park today with that bruise!" I said, stomping my foot. "You know you can't. Come with us. You've got nothing to lose."

Kerry got to her feet and followed me downstairs. I whispered to Mama. She touched Kerry's shoulder. "I'm sorry to hear what happened, Kerry. Elsie's right. Come with us. You're a child of God. You need to believe that." We were just going in the door to the Great Auditorium when Kerry bolted. She disappeared between two tents.

I listened carefully to the sermon this time, wondering what it might have meant to Kerry. When the minister said something about the body being a temple, about keeping it holy and healthy, I could hardly breathe. The sermon was written for Kerry! Goosebumps climbed my arms. Goosebumps from God, I thought with a smile. I tried telling Kerry about it later after tea, but she just walked away.

Days passed and we were well into August. One Friday I went to visit Grandpa.

"Big news today," he said. "Sam Lawrence came back from the convalescent home in Spring Lake. He's in a wheel chair with a big cast on his leg."

"Maybe I'll go say hello," I said. I found the Lawrence yard full of well-wishers. Mrs. Lawrence chatted with friends, her back facing the sidewalk. Her erect posture fairly shouted, "Good-bye to you, Miss," but I chose to ignore it. Sam sat on the porch in a rocking chair, his leg propped on a stool. The chair with wheels was next to him, piled high with presents. Sarah leaned on Sam's arm. She pointed to the package on his lap.

"Look, Sammy, Tootsie Rolls and Hershey bars!" she exclaimed. "Can I have some?" A pretty girl with blonde hair offered Sam a yellow box that could only mean Whitman's chocolates. Oh, dear, I had no gift. I walked away.

Grandpa was inside his tent when I returned, talking quietly with someone. Who was visiting? I peeked inside the flap.

"Aha! She *is* here!" It was Father!

I jumped backwards, but Father grabbed my skirt and held on. "Elsie," he said, "I won't hurt you. I'm fine. Look at me. I'm fine."

I looked into his eyes. He let go of my skirt. His face looked older. His clean-shaven cheeks sagged and his eyes were sunk in dark hollows. He smelled of something pleasant—soapy and spicy. I moved closer. Then he smiled and stretched out his arms. My heart thumped as I stepped tentatively into his awkward hug.

"I came to see you and your mother," he said. "Your Grandfather told me you both work in Long Branch, but here you are." His voice hardened. "Now tell me where you really work!"

"Elsie, don't say a word," Grandpa commanded. "I tell you what, Horace, if you stay sober another whole week, I'll let you see Elsie again. And if you stay sober the week after that, then I'll tell Fannie and let her decide whether to see you or not."

Father's head fell forward and he began rubbing his hair and muttering. I stepped away from him. I pulled out the wooden box and found the temperance pledges.

"Father, I got this for you." He lifted his head expectantly.

"What's that?" he said.

"It's a temperance pledge. If you sign it, you promise to never, ever drink liquor. again. Then we can all live together! And be happy! Will you sign it?"

"I don't need no stupid temperance pledge! Where's your mother? What I need is cash. What I need is my job back. That's what I need. Not some stupid piece of paper." He grabbed the pledge, crumpled it in a ball and threw it on the floor.

"Elsie, go in the kitchen, please," Grandpa said. He motioned for me to run out the back door. I did.

Ingeborg stopped me in the parlor. "Two letters for you, Elsie."

I tore open Mama's letter. She had a bad summer cold and wouldn't be coming Sunday. I kept reading.

I hate to disappoint you, Elsie, but I'm fever-ish and tired. I'm working so many hours, but we need the money. I think I caught the cold last night when the night watchman didn't unlock the door until ten o'clock. I had fallen asleep on the floor with the others when in he walks, stinking of alcohol. He waved away our protests and pushed us out the door. He didn't even check our pockets. I told him I was going to tell the foreman. 'Go ahead,' he snarled. 'I can make your life so hard, you'll beg to quit.' I crept home, too tired to eat the supper Minnie had saved.

Poor Mama. It wasn't fair she worked so hard, while Father did nothing. I opened the second letter. The return address read New York College Settlement House.

Dear Miss Shaw,

Thank you for your letter. It was interesting to hear that my graduation poem was mentioned at the WCTU conference. I should like to visit Ocean Grove some day. I've heard it's a beautiful seaside town with wonderful concerts and Sunday services.

I am truly sorry to hear of your family's troubles. You are not alone, believe me. We see your story over and over again here at the settlement house. I would be very glad for your help after school if you're quite sure your mother doesn't need you. I'm afraid we can't pay you, and I understand if you must find a paying position. The number of immigrants flooding into New York grows every day, and you sound like a mature girl just right to help us with the children. Come see me when you return to the city.

Yours truly,
Miss Alice Paul

CHAPTER EIGHT

Parading with a Purpose

Perambulators at the Asbury Park Baby Parade

"Grandpa, do you know anyone looking for a girl to watch children in the evening?" It was Saturday, and I was adding my latest pay envelope to the growing pile in the rosemaling box.

"Why do you want to work at night, Elsie?" Grandpa asked.

"Well, if I earn extra money, maybe Mama won't have to work such long days."

"I'll ask around, Elsie," he said, "but I know your mother doesn't want you working day and night. It would please her if you enjoyed the ocean and the fresh air."

"I will, Grandpa. I will."

And I did. The weather was sunny and dry the following week, and I sat on the sand every day to read. I loved being down by the water. It was so much cooler. But I still didn't bathe in the sea. I had no bathing dress, and to tell the truth, I was a little afraid of the surf. The waves could be rough, especially when they rolled in at high tide. Bathers grabbed for the ropes to keep their balance. Emily came with me one day, and we got our feet wet collecting shells at the water's edge. What fun!

On Saturday, Mama appeared as breakfast was ending. She stood in the doorway, her face as white as bone. She wore a new sailor-style dress of white and navy blue.

"Are you train-sick, Mama?" I asked. "Why are you here on Saturday?"

"No, I'm not train-sick," she said. "The truth is, I'm taking a holiday from work. The night watchman didn't let us out until nearly midnight Thursday. I told the foreman yesterday that I was too sick to work. Besides, the newspaper said Asbury Park's famous Baby Parade is today. I'm hoping we can see it. I don't even care about the money we'll lose."

Mrs. Lewis came from the kitchen. "Well, how wonderful to see you, Fannie," she exclaimed. "And what a delightful dress. Did you make it?"

"No, my friend Minnie bought it for me on sale at the dress shop where she works. It was damaged, but I mended it."

"It's just the thing for the big parade," said Mrs. Lewis. "It's a huge event and I'd already arranged for my niece to come help me this weekend. I can spare Elsie until after the parade. Mr. Heines might like to see the parade too."

"Yes, I plan to go get him. Thank you, Mrs. Lewis," Mama said.

"Oh, call me Maude, please."

"Thank you, Maude. You know, Elsie and I were in the parade back in 1898. She was six years old, and such a darling." I squirmed. Who wanted to hear this?

"I'll bet she was," said Mrs. Lewis. "How did you dress her?"

"Like Mistress Mary, from Mother Goose. You know, 'Mistress Mary, quite contrary, how does your garden grow? With silver bells and cockle shells and pretty maids all in a row.'" Mama twirled me around like a ballerina. "Her father built a little white picket fence inside a red wagon. I piled it high with garden flowers and pulled it along the boardwalk. Elsie stood in the wagon, pretending to water the flowers. She wore a pretty pink dress and white ruffled bloomers on her legs. My Mama sewed them. And a white bonnet with pink ribbons. Do you remember, Elsie?"

"Yes. I wore that dress a lot, but I hated the bloomers!

Did we win a prize?"

"Why, yes, we did. A little silver loving cup, engraved with the year. I wonder where that went?"

"The prizes are getting grander every year," said Mrs. Lewis. "You know, the prizes for the very first parade in 1890 were simple boxes of salt water taffy. Imagine that? Today they give away sets of china and silver platters, jewelry, watches." Grandpa walked in.

"Well, look who's here for his second cup of coffee," boomed Mrs. Lewis.

"Fannie!" he exclaimed, "What a surprise." He hugged her tightly.

After coffee, tea and muffins, Mrs. Lewis ordered us to leave. "Now off you go," she sniffled, wiping her nose with a handkerchief. "It's a day of fun for the lot of you."

The Asbury Park boardwalk overflowed with spectators. The grandstands were draped with bunting. Every seat was filled. A wheel chair at the far end of the grandstand caught my eye. It was Sam! I waved and he waved back.

"Who's that waving?" Mama asked.

"That's Sam Lawrence," I said. "His father's behind him."

"So that's the boy I keep hearing about," said Grandpa. "He broke his leg trying to rescue his little sister from the lake."

"Oh my," said Mama. "He was successful, I hope."

"Not really," I said. "His cousin Teddy saved Sarah. Sam broke his leg trying."

"Teddy's the boy who shook hands with President Roosevelt, Fannie," said Grandpa. "Some of the President's courage must have rubbed off on the little guy. It's been quite the story here all summer."

"Look, Sam's waving again," Mama said.

I waved back, and Sam smiled. At me!

"Hmm...I'll have to meet this Sam," Mama murmured.

"Not now, Fannie," said Grandpa. "The boardwalk is filling up fast. We've got to find a place to stand." Finally, we found an empty spot. My heart floated with happiness. How wonderful to be just another normal family, standing on the sidelines, waiting for a parade to start. How wonderful to see Sam smile. At me.

Boys blew long brass horns, and pretty girls stretched across the boardwalk holding a banner that read, "15th Annual Asbury Park Baby Parade." A band followed, playing a march that made my toes tap. The parade of wicker perambulators began. Mothers pushed prams covered with so many flowers it was hard to find the babies inside. A boy in a sailor suit and hat sat in a small red rowboat set on wheels. Next came a goat pulling a red, white, and blue cart with two little girls inside. The goat stopped every few steps, planting its hooves like stubborn roots on the wooden planks. The father tugged on the leash, red-faced and sweating.

A brown and white pony pranced behind the goat cart with a Rough Rider boy sitting in the saddle. Every time he waved his wooden sword and yelled, "Charge!" the spectators roared their approval.

"Atta boy," yelled Grandpa. "Charge up that hill, just like Roosevelt!"

I pulled Mama's arm. "Sam's a Rough Rider too. He marches and sings with them. At least he did before he broke his leg." All Mama said was, "Hmmm."

More decorated prams rolled by, then four beautiful white horses pulled an elaborate float called "The Royal Court of the 1905 Baby Parade." It reminded me of the Children's Festival. A king and queen sat on thrones, their crowns sparkling in the sun. Girls in long gowns stood on each side, their arms draped with flowers.

Mama clapped and smiled like a little girl. I hadn't seen that smile this whole sad summer. "Elsie, it's beautiful, isn't it?" she exclaimed. "I'd love to sew gorgeous gowns like those! Maybe I will someday. I'm so glad I skipped work to see this with you."

More prams and floats went by. One float had King Neptune with his trident, surrounded by beautiful mermaids. Suddenly, a very plain brown perambulator appeared. It was pushed by an equally plain young woman in a black skirt and white shirtwaist. Not a flower in sight. Even the baby was hidden. Was it sleeping?

The woman reached into her pram and pulled out a circle of wide yellow ribbon. She lifted it up and over her head. It fell down on one shoulder and draped across her chest. She turned from side to side, letting everyone read the white letters sewn on the ribbon, "Votes for Women."

Her act was so surprising, so shocking, that people fell silent. Again she lifted a ribbon from the pram. A young woman standing nearby walked to the pram, took the ribbon, put it on, and turned so we could read it. Someone started booing. Someone else began to applaud. Another ribbon was lifted up, and a stout older woman came forward, removed her flowered hat, put the ribbon on, replaced her hat, and marched.

My heart leaped and began beating in my throat. Suffragists! Another ribbon was thrust in the air, and my feet moved forward before my brain could stop them. I reached for the ribbon and put it on. Hundreds of people stared, but I didn't flinch. Women needed the vote. I'd heard all the reasons this summer. I held my head high.

"Elsie, Elsie," Mama called, running to catch up. I reached into the pram and pulled up another ribbon. Mama put it on! More and more women joined us. The cheering and jeering got louder and louder.

"Go get a husband and have a real baby!" yelled a man.

Another shouted, "Go back home where you belong!"

A woman yelled, "Women and politics don't mix! You're a disgrace to your husbands."

The woman pushing the pram started chanting, "Votes for women. Votes for women. Votes for women." We joined her, and amazingly, so did many spectators. The naysayers could not drown out the chanters: "Votes for women. Votes for women."

There were no more ribbons in the pram, but that didn't stop women from joining our march. The measured words of the chant matched our marching feet. Mama and I held hands, and I'm sure it's all that kept me tethered to the ground, for I felt as light as a cloud.

The grandstand lay ahead. Police stood on both sides of the boardwalk. Would they stop us? Embarrass us? Send us to the lock-up? None of it mattered. I felt pure and clean and alive, really alive, for the first time in a long time.

"Elsie, Elsie," called a familiar voice. It was Sam. He and his father waved again. Dumbstruck, I waved back.

Suddenly the policemen linked arms across the board-walk, blocking our path.

A stocky man in the middle spoke. "All right now, ladies, if I may call you that after your very unlady-like performance. Who's the leader here? What's your parade number?" The woman with the pram showed her number, 76. "And where's your baby?" He pulled the baby blanket back. "Just as I thought. No baby—no marching in the baby parade. With your attitude, Miss, I'll wager this empty pram is the only one you'll ever push." The policemen laughed. "You'll stay with us until the parade is over. The rest of you," he raised his voice, "are free to go back to your families. Any further trouble and you will be detained."

"That's fine with me," said the woman with the pram. "Thank you, ladies. I think we made a grand statement today. Go back to your families now and enjoy the parade. Keep your banners. Use them to continue our fight for the vote. Keep the dream alive! God bless you." We watched the rest of the parade, waiting for Grandpa.

"That was so exciting!" Mama exclaimed. "Did you know that was going to happen?"

"No, I didn't," I said, "but I heard suffragists give speeches this summer. And...I did it for you, Mama, because you work in a sweatshop. The suffragists said we need to change the labor laws."

"And I marched for you, Elsie. I hope one day you'll be able to vote, even if I don't live to see it happen. Oh, I can't wait to tell Minnie what we did. She'll be so proud of us."

We basked in the glow of our march all that night.

Mrs. Lewis insisted on taking us out for a fish dinner at the Albatross Hotel and hearing the whole story. Later, Mama and I slept on the floor in Grandpa's tent. Our new-found courage squashed any fears of Father. I woke up to the wonderful sound of her voice, "Good morning, Elsie Sunshine." I showed her all the money I'd saved in the rosemaling box.

"You've earned so much!" Mama exclaimed. "Grandpa told me how you save every penny. We're going to be just fine this fall, you'll see." She smoothed my hair back and tied it with a white ribbon. "I'm proud of you in so many ways, Elsie. You're growing into a wonderful young woman."

Grandpa fried eggs and bacon. Phillip brought over a basket of blueberry muffins from Mrs. Lewis. "She says to stay with your mother until tea time, Elsie, then come to work," he said. We dug into the food.

"You're too thin, Fannie," Grandpa said. "You're still my little girl, and I order you to eat another muffin." I decided to tell Mama about Father's visit. How he looked sober. How he crumpled up the temperance pledge I gave him and threw it on the ground.

"That reminds me," said Grandpa. He handed me the wrinkled pledge. "I smoothed it out best I could."

"Thank you, Grandpa. I still have the second pledge too. The girl who gave them to me said it sometimes takes more than one pledge to help a person stop drinking."

"Elsie, don't get your heart too set on it," Mama said. "Your father's tried before to stop. We have to concentrate on taking care of ourselves." She took a deep breath. "Now, I don't want to talk about your father any more. I want to celebrate all the money you and I have saved. I think we'll have enough for an apartment, not just a room. It won't be long now, Elsie!" I didn't mention working with Alice Paul at the settlement house. It might not even happen if I needed to earn money for the apartment.

After church and a quick lunch with ice cream at Day's, I walked Mama back to the train station in Asbury Park. She climbed aboard and waved good-bye. What I remember most is how pink her cheeks were, and how brightly her eyes sparkled.

CHAPTER NINE

"There's Been an Accident!"

A stylish sailor blouse and skirt to wear by the sea

T he weather turned hot the following week. Mrs. Lewis complained loudly as she mopped her dripping face. The coolest places were the boardwalk and the beach. Tourists crowded both, lingering outdoors long into the night. All over town, upstairs porches were turned into bedrooms. Sleeping porches, they called them. Kerry and I dragged our bedding out to the tiny porch on the fourth floor and slept under the stars. Every night I God-blessed Reverend Osborn for planting Ocean Grove on this miraculous, mosquito-free land.

It was hard to read Kerry. She was withdrawn, quiet. Not a peaceful quiet, but not an angry one either. We worked and slept beside each other, but there was a distance in our togetherness.

Thursday morning I awoke to another perfect blue-sky-white-cloud day. I could almost hear Mama's cheery, "Good morning, Elsie Sunshine." I worked breakfast, then tea. It was late afternoon when I took a book out to the porch and plopped into a rocking chair. Grandpa appeared suddenly, pulling himself slowly up the stairs. A young woman followed him. Minnie! Mama's friend from New York. What was she doing here? Where was Mama?

"We'll be right back, Elsie," Grandpa said. "I need to find Mrs. Lewis." His words were muffled. Minnie kept her eyes fixed on the steps. The corners of her mouth turned down, like some strange upside-down smile. Her lips quivered. I stopped rocking. The book fell from my hands. Minutes passed.

Mrs. Lewis came to the door. "Elsie, come inside, please." I followed her, my body shivering in the heat. We went into her private office. She shut the door and sat beside Grandpa.

"Elsie," he began, "there's been an accident."

"Where?" I asked.

"In New York City. It'll be in the newspapers tomorrow. A fire. A terrible fire."

"Where?" I asked again.

Grandpa put his face in his hands and sobbed. Mrs. Lewis wrapped her arm around his shoulders.

"I guess it's my sad duty to tell you, Elsie," said Minnie. She moved her mouth, but no sound came out. She cleared her throat. "There was a fire very early this morning at a shirtwaist factory. The one where your mother worked." She paused, giving me time to absorb her words. Worked. Past tense of work. No longer working.

"No, no. Not Mama! Is she hurt?"

Minnie squeezed me tightly. "She's gone, Elsie. Three people died in the fire."

"No, she's not! She's not!" My hands started shaking, then my whole body.

Minnie loosened her hold and spoke softly. "I heard that the fire started in the basement, after midnight. The front door was locked when the firemen arrived. They smashed it down. Three bodies...oh God, I can't say anymore," she sobbed. I waited, my body as stiff as a statue. Minnie blew her nose. "Three bodies were found near the door," she said slowly. "No identities have been released."

"See, it's *not* Mama!" I yelled, stepping away from this strange, hateful Minnie.

Why was she trying to hurt me? "Mama escaped out a window. I know she did. We're going to live together next month. She promised."

Minnie lifted my chin and stared into my eyes. "Elsie, your mother never came back to our room last night.

I heard fire bells, but I paid no mind. I hear them all the time. Your Mama worked overtime every night. She probably didn't tell you. She didn't want you to worry. This morning...her bed was empty." She paused. "And I know for a fact the building where she worked has iron bars on all first floor windows."

Pain shot through my heart. I bent over as deep, gulping sobs wracked my body. "I don't believe it," I cried. "Why would this happen?"

"I think we know why," Minnie said gruffly. "It's because the owner locked his workers inside. Afraid they'd steal his stupid needles and thread. He treated them like thieves. And his night watchman was a drunk. Unlocking the door later and later for overtime workers. They never complained—afraid they'd lose their jobs.

"Two of your mother's friends stopped working overtime because of the night watchman," she continued. "I don't think he ever arrived last night. Sleeping off his whiskey when the fire started, I'll wager. We'll see what the newspapers say tomorrow, but this was no accident. This was murder."

Those were the last words I heard before crashing to the floor in a dead faint.

The next thing I knew, sun was shining on my face. I smelled coffee and oatmeal, felt carpet beneath me. Remembrance struck like an arrow: everyone talking and talking, telling me Mama was dead. But she wasn't. *Mama*, I prayed silently, *please be alive! Please, please! Smell that oatmeal? You're right, Mrs. Lewis is sweet on*

Grandpa. Come see for yourself. My unspoken words comforted me. Mama was alive. I felt her nearness. I could talk to her.

Grandpa lay on the divan. Minnie was scrunched in a pink upholstered chair. Grandpa stretched. "Boy, that smells good," he said. He saw me on the floor and his face twisted in pain. Mrs. Lewis came from her kitchen with coffee cups and bowls of oatmeal.

"Glad to see you're awake, Elsie," she said. "I woke you briefly last night and slipped you one of my sleeping pills. Didn't want you waking up in the middle of the night."

Minnie awoke and left without a word. Minutes later she came back and handed me the morning edition of *The New York Times*. "Shirtwaist Factory Fire!" read one of the headlines. I skimmed down to three names. One was Mrs. Frances H. Shaw. The paper slipped from my fingers, and I wailed, long and hard.

CHAPTER TEN

Fannie's Secret

Horse-drawn carriages wait for passengers at the train station

"I'm going out to hire a carriage to New York," Grandpa said. "I hate riding trains. I'm always train-sick. I'll be sick today for sure. My stomach's already churning. My heart's racing. Oh, my poor, poor Fannie. What an awful day." He left.

Ingeborg came in with a Western Union envelope. A telegram for me, she said. In the tenements, a telegram meant bad news. Someone in the old country had died, most likely. No one wanted to open a telegram. A family would hand it around until one brave soul opened and read it. I already knew my bad news. Nothing could be worse. I tore the envelope open.

"DEAR ELSBETH STOP VERY SORRY ABOUT MOTHER STOP COME HERE WITH GRANDFA-THER STOP CAN BURY MOTHER HERE AT HER CHURCH STOP LOVE PASTOR ELLISEN STOP"

I went upstairs to pack. When I returned, the apartment was empty. I shivered, feeling hard and cold and alone, like a statue of carved ice. A voice in my head whispered, *Sherry will warm you. Take a sip.* No, I answered. *You deserve it. Your mother's dead.* I opened the cabinet, found two bottles, and took a mouthful from the opened one. Again, the burning liquid bored deep inside. My icy heart was untouched. Against all my beliefs in right and wrong, I slipped the bottle into my satchel.

Grandpa returned. I showed him the telegram. "So we'll go to your church," he said. Minnie, Grandpa and I climbed into the carriage. Mrs. Lewis came running from Britannia, the bib of her apron bobbling up and down every which way with the effort. She handed me a large bouquet of pink and white roses. The stems were wrapped in a wet towel.

"Your Mum loved my roses," she said tearfully. "Take these to her. Be careful of thorns." She waved good-bye. The horses clip-clopped along at a steady pace. Grandpa puffed on his pipe. He and Minnie were quiet, lost in thought. To avoid any thinking of my own, I counted cows in all the small farms we passed in New Jersey.

We arrived at my Orchard Street neighborhood by late afternoon. I was surprised how dark everything looked. Tall tenement buildings blocked the sunshine, sending deep shadows over the streets and sidewalks. Everything looked drab and gray. There was no green in this strange orchard, except for a few vegetables piled in pushcarts. Peddlers jostled for space with pedestrians, horses, buggies and trolley cars. I pictured the sunny green lawn on Ocean Pathway with a pang.

A newsboy shouted, "Fire in factory! Read all about it!" He waved a paper up at us with a big smile. Grandpa shook his head, but Minnie bought one. The boy was so close, I could have opened the carriage door and kicked that smile right off his face.

I directed the driver to our church. Minnie and Grandpa went to the pastor's office. I went downstairs with the roses, where I knew the ladies would be cooking food for the funeral. Just like Mama used to do. My body trembled as they circled around me, their familiar faces and loving arms trying to comfort me.

Mrs. O'Brien took the roses. A thorn jabbed her thumb, beading it with blood. She wiped it on the white dishtowel covering the stems, and suddenly I felt dizzy. I saw Mama's bloody dishtowel pushing through dark pine trees. I reached out to steady myself, and there was Molly! I grabbed her arm and erupted in tears. We sat together, holding hands, until I stopped crying. Grandpa and Minnie walked in.

"Everything is set," Grandpa said. "Pastor Ellisen was

able to identify Fannie's...body...for the police. I'm grateful he did that. He's giving us a spot behind the church to bury her. I've chosen a plain wood coffin. I'll get a headstone later." He stopped and blew his nose. "It's a comfort knowing my daughter will rest in the arms of her church, but oh, there's nothing worse than burying your own child."

He lowered himself onto a straight-backed wooden chair. "There'll be no viewing," he struggled to continue, "due to...the circumstances of her death. She'll be buried tomorrow after the service."

"I'm glad to hear you're comforted, Mr. Heines," said Pastor Ellisen, coming into the kitchen. "Your daughter was a special person, and I've decided to share something with all of you that Fannie told me never to tell. But now that she's gone, I feel it's important you know Fannie's secret."

Secret? Mama had a secret?

"Elsie," he said, "did you know your mother sewed baby clothes for immigrants?" I shook my head. "Well, she did. Many newborns are birthed at sea, or on Ellis Island. The mothers have little to dress them in. The ones who land in our neighborhood are supplied with the bare basics at College Settlement House. But Fannie gave them something extra. She gave them beauty.

"Ladies," he continued, "remember how I pestered you for scraps of material? Any leftover pretty fabric? I gave it all to Fannie and she turned it into tiny dresses, night gowns, blankets, and bibs. Charming and adorable. Every Friday she'd take a few pieces to the settlement house. Sometimes she met the mothers and held their babies. She really enjoyed that."

I couldn't believe what I was hearing. "But I thought she was sewing piece work for the factories!" I exclaimed. "That's how she earned money."

"She did that too," said the pastor. "She sewed piece work for hours every day. It fed your family. She called her baby clothes 'night work.' She'd do it while you and your father slept. She didn't want him finding out about it. Afraid he'd make her stop. I don't think she slept very much."

I ached, thinking of the nights I'd fallen asleep listening to Mama sew in the front room. Heard the steady thumping of the pedal as she pumped it with her foot, up and down, up and down. The faster she pumped, the faster the needle whirred across the fabric. The glow of her kerosene lamp was the last thing I saw before falling asleep on my cot in the kitchen.

"Another reason I'm telling you," Pastor Ellisen said, "is because a woman from the settlement house asked to speak at Fannie's funeral."

"From the settlement house?" I asked. "Is her name Alice Paul?"

"I'm sorry," said the pastor, "I don't remember her name, but I'll get it for you. I told her she could speak, unless the family objects. The important thing is that your mother's secret is shared. Her example can inspire us all." The room fell silent. A lump grew in my throat. I tried to swallow it away.

"Has anyone seen my father?" I asked in a tiny voice I hardly recognized.

Molly took my hand. "I saw him the day he was

thrown out of your apartment for good. The landlord had already tossed whatever was left inside out the window. The sidewalk was a mess. Your father grabbed what he could, then disappeared."

"We heard he's over in the Bowery," the pastor added. "That's only a few blocks away, I know, but it's a whole different world. He could be living in a flophouse, or on the streets with the other drunks. I doubt he even knows about your mother. I have friends at the Bowery Mission keeping a look-out for him."

Grandpa sagged in his chair. I hid my face on Molly's shoulder.

"I apologize if I've added to your pain," said Pastor Ellisen, "but you need to know the truth. I'm praying we find Horace soon and get him the help he needs. Elsie, you always have a church family here. And so does your father. We are all so very sorry about this terrible accident."

I lifted my head and yelled, "It was no accident—it was murder!"

"What did you say?" asked the pastor.

"Murder!" I shouted into the shocked silence.

"Well, I don't think anyone intentionally murdered your mother," he said. "I know you're upset and you've every right to be. It's a terrible..."

"No!" I interrupted. "Mama wrote and told me she worked late. She *told* me she was locked in! She *told* me the night watchman was a drunk, getting there later every night. He *should* have been on time. He *should* have!"

Minnie put her arm around me. "I'm to blame," she

said. "I told her it was murder, because I believe it was. Negligent murder. We've got to stop these sweatshops from abusing their workers!"

"Yes, Minnie, I know that's how you feel, but now is not the time," said the pastor gently. "First we'll help the grieving family, then we can fight for social justice."

"I wish you was here yesterday when a reporter came by, Minnie," said one of the ladies. "Wanted to know where Frances Shaw lived. Snooping around for quotes. I told him nothing. He might come back for the funeral."

"I'll be happy to give him an earful," Minnie said.

One of Mama's friends handed me three plates of food. "We have plenty for tomorrow," she said. "Take this for your supper tonight."

"And you two are staying with me," said Minnie. "I can't go back to that empty room alone. The landlady won't complain about extra boarders if she saves money not feeding me tonight."

I spent another night on another floor, this time between Minnie's bed and the one Grandpa snored on— Mama's bed. Light from the hallway slipped in under the door, outlining Mama's night dress hanging on a hook. I reached up to her nightstand and found her hair brush. I held it to my cheek, startled to breathe in Mama's familiar scent. It clung to the brush along with a few strands of hair. I laid my head down and silent tears rolled onto Mama's pillow. How could I possibly sleep?

Then I remembered. Quietly, quietly I reached into my satchel and pulled out the bottle of sherry. I swallowed gulp after gulp, ignoring the burning and craving it at the same time. I put the bottle away and laid down, my head spinning itself to sleep. Mama's hairbrush was still in my hand when I awoke in the morning.

The funeral passed in a hazy blur. My head throbbed with pain. My stomach churned with nausea. Why now? I thought angrily. Didn't I have enough trouble without worrying about throwing up?

Mama's coffin was nailed shut before it came into the church. Grandpa was firm about that. "Remember her at the baby parade, Elsie—how beautiful she looked and how happy you made her that day."

We sang "Nearer My God to Thee." The organ notes pounded like a hammer on my skull. The roses from Mrs. Lewis sat in a large vase at one end of the coffin. Was that where Mama's head lay? I couldn't bear the thought. I tried to concentrate as the pastor spoke about Mama's eternal life. How there was no end to eternity. How her love of God and generous spirit would be rewarded in heaven. She lived with the angels now, he said, and we could all learn from her example.

I kept looking at the door. Would Father come? Would he smell soapy and clean like the last time I saw him? Oh, no! Suddenly I remembered—Father had lots of morning headaches! Sometimes he retched right in the kitchen sink. He'd drink his coffee, growling and cursing, then lurch off to work. Did the sherry give me this headache? Was I turning into him?

The lady from the settlement house spoke. It wasn't Alice Paul. I forgot her name as soon as I heard it. Again I was amazed by the story of Mama and the baby clothes. The congregation sang, but I could not. The elders carried the coffin outside. I laid my cheek on the wood, crying, "Mama, Mama," until Grandpa pulled me into his arms. The coffin was lowered beneath a tree with thin branches drooping to the ground. A willow tree, Grandpa said. A weeping willow.

Mama's friends each threw a shovelful of dirt on the coffin. When the shovel was handed to me, I threw a piece of my broken heart into the grave along with the dirt. We all went back inside, to a meal I couldn't eat and hugs I couldn't return. Later, Minnie and I took the roses outside. The gravedigger had finished his job. We spread the flowers across the mound of fresh dirt. I slipped a pink rosebud into my pocket.

Minnie wanted us to stay another night, but Grandpa asked for the carriage. His face was damp and gray. We climbed in and drove away. I waved to Molly until we turned a corner and she was gone.

Grandpa fell asleep soon after we left. Time passed, and the sky grew darker. Again, we rolled past the farms, invisible now, except for a few lit windows in the farmhouses. I sucked in my breath when the driver turned the horses east, toward the sea. Memories of Mama and I escaping were everywhere. Wait! Without Mama, where would I live? I sat bolt upright in the carriage. How would I survive? I'd seen abandoned street urchins, digging through trash cans. Could that happen to me? Soon I smelled the ocean. Tonight it smelled like danger.

I calmed myself by remembering how Mama always called me her poet. She had said it again that night, when I compared the headlamps of a motor car to tiny moons. I'd laughed then, but now I wanted more than anything to be her poet. "Mama," I whispered, "I'll write you a poem, I promise."

I tried rhyming a few words in my head, but nothing worked. I tried comparing things. Nothing. Everything was what it was. The sea was the sea. A box was only a box, even if it held the dearest person in the world. I pulled the rosebud from my pocket. And a rose was just a rose.

We reached the pounding sea and turned south. The moon was full tonight, spilling a silver pathway over the dark sea. The man in the moon looked into my eyes. *Come to me,* he seemed to say. *Walk up my pathway. I'm eternal—like your mother.* My eyes closed and I fell into the small eternity of dreamless sleep.

CHAPTER ELEVEN

Decisions

The Angel of Victory statue, built in 1878

"Whoa now, whoa, fellas," said the driver loudly, waking Grandpa and me up. We were at Britannia. Mrs. Lewis leaped from her porch. How long had she'd been waiting, I wondered? Grandpa paid the driver, and climbed the porch steps. At the top, he clutched his chest and toppled over.

"Gunther!" cried Mrs. Lewis. "Are you ill? Speak to me!" Grandpa was silent. His legs draped over the steps. "Crikey!" she yelled. "Elsie, run. Get an Adam's ale."

"A what?" I asked. Grandpa hadn't moved. My hands started to shake.

"A glass of water! And bloody hurry!" Suddenly Hank stepped out of the shadows alongside Britannia.

"Hank, what are you doing here at this hour?" Mrs. Lewis asked. "Never mind. You're perfect. Can you carry Mr. Heines inside? We'll put him in my office. Elsie, are you daft? Get the water."

Hank lifted Grandpa as if he were a rag doll. When I came back with the water, Grandpa was stretched out on the divan with his head propped against a pile of pink velvet cushions. His eyes were open!

"Here," said Mrs. Lewis, putting the glass to his lips, "can you swallow?" Grandpa nodded and took a sip.

"I'm fine, Maude," he said. "Shaky, but fine. It just felt like my heart stopped beating for a bit. That's all."

"That's *all?*" Mrs. Lewis said. "Hank, run to Doctor Alday's on Main Avenue. Where you got stitches on your thumb, remember? Go to the back door. Ask him to come quickly. Oh—if anyone stops you at this late hour, tell them I sent you. Get one of my calling cards on your way out, and show them that."

"Yes,m," said Hank. He left. I curled up on the floor by Grandpa's head. Mrs. Lewis took off his shoes and tie. She unbuttoned his shirt collar. She fussed with the pillows.

When the doctor came, I went out to the porch. Please

God, I prayed silently, not Grandpa too. Creak, went my rocker. Not Grandpa too. Creak. I must have rocked a million creaks and prayed a million prayers before Dr. Alday and Mrs. Lewis walked out.

"I think he'll be fine, Mrs. Lewis," said the doctor. "From what you tell me, he's had a terrible shock today burying his daughter. And the way he describes it, I don't think he had a heart attack. He may have a problem with heart rhythm. It could be serious. Let him rest now, then come in for a full examination. I left medicine. It should help him sleep."

Thank you, God, I prayed silently.

"Mr. Heines is a lucky man to have a friend like you, Mrs. Lewis," continued the doctor. "You should get some rest as well." Hank walked out on the porch. "Good to see you again, Hank," said Dr. Alday, shaking his hand. "Glad to see your thumb healed so well. Good night, everyone."

Mrs. Lewis heaved a powerful sigh. "Thank you, Doctor," she said. "And thank you, Hank. Why did you say you were here so late?"

"Just uneasy, Miz Lewis. Philip and Patience gone to her parents in Freehold. Elsie and her Grandpaw in New York City. You looking so sad. I decided to hang around. Quiet-like."

"You certainly were; I had no idea," she said. "I'll pay you extra this week for your time."

"No need for that. I did what I wanted. You go to sleep now. I'll be here 'til Philip's back."

"Thank you, Hank. I can't thank you enough. Good night, Elsie. I hope you sleep, luv, after this terrible day.

You can tell me about the funeral tomorrow, dear girl."
Her shoulders slumped as she opened the door. She
looked nothing like the brisk woman who sailed through
each day fully in charge. No, the wind had shifted, her
sails were empty, and her whole body drooped.

I crawled into bed. Kerry was asleep. My head ran
moving pictures of Mama's funeral over and over. Suddenly I remembered my satchel, and the bottle of sherry.
I'd left it on the floor by Grandpa! Guilt chased my nightmares all night long.

I awoke to dim, gray light. The sun hadn't risen. I rolled
over to go back to sleep, and memory jolted me—Mama!
Sleep was impossible now, so I slipped downstairs and
out on the porch. The sky changed from gray to yellow to
morning blue. The ocean reflected the rising sun. Waves
sparkled like jewels. How much longer would I live with
this beauty? Where would I go when summer ended? No
answers came, and I began another day in my hateful
new life without Mama.

I spoke to no one as we served breakfast. It was easier
that way. Patience fussed, offering me food. Kerry was
quiet and Emily tearful. They asked a few questions,
then gave up. I went to Mrs. Lewis's apartment after
breakfast. Grandpa was sitting up on the couch, his feet
on the floor! He held out his arms, and I ran into them.

"Elsie, I'm sorry I scared you," he said weakly.

"It's all right. How are you?"

"Well, it's hard to answer. I'm terribly sad, and sick,
and hopeful all at once."

"Hopeful?" I asked. "What are you hopeful about?"

"You tell her, Maude."

"Gunther," said Mrs. Lewis, "you're doing just fine."

Grandpa took a deep breath. "Well, Mrs. Lewis and I have been good friends this summer. She lost her husband and I lost my wife, and we're both not getting any younger. At our age, two is better than one. So now you know."

"Um, know what, Grandpa?"

Mrs. Lewis chuckled. "Forgive me at such a sad time, but you are a funny man, Gunther Heines, if you think that tells your granddaughter anything."

"What?" Grandpa exclaimed. "I told her we're getting married, didn't I?"

I jumped to my feet. "You are? When?"

"Right away," Grandpa said. "Mrs. Lewis wants to care for me here in her home. And we'd like you to come live with us, Elsie. I'm selling my farmhouse and moving in here. We're going to knock down a few walls and make a second bedroom for you. It's all settled."

"It's all settled?" I repeated. The room seemed to tilt, and I grabbed the arm of the divan. Mrs. Lewis reached for my other arm.

"Poor Elsie," she said. "It's too soon after your Mama's death for wedding plans. In fact, it's indecently soon. We know we're breaking all the rules of etiquette for proper mourning of a loved one. But your Grandpa needs someone to take care of him, and this is the best way. The wedding will be simple and small. And we're not just two pigs in a poke, you know."

"Pigs? What pigs?" I asked.

"Blimey! It means we know what we're getting into," Mrs. Lewis exclaimed. She pulled herself up straight. "It means we've gotten to know each other. Our eyes are wide open. And we don't want the gossip-mongers spreading scandals about us."

She patted Grandpa's arm. "I can't bear to think of Gunther alone in that Pennsylvania house all winter long. Even if you lived there with him, it's a big responsibility for a school girl." Me, live in a farmhouse? In the country? I had never, ever thought of that.

"Um, I don't know what to say," I muttered. "Mama said you were sweet on each other. Guess she was right. I...I'm going for a walk." I raced outside and down the porch steps, nearly crashing into a girl and older woman walking up the stairs.

"Remember me, Elsie?" the girl said. "Amelia Shirm? From the temperance meeting? This is my mother."

"Oh, yes. Sorry, Amelia. I'm just not myself right now."

"Of course you're not, you poor dear girl," said Mrs. Shirm. She pulled me into a warm, motherly hug. I stiffened in her arms. "Go ahead and cry, dear," Mrs. Shirm murmured. "We came to tell you how sorry we are about the fire, and your mother. A terrible, terrible thing." Tears gathered in my eyes, but I clamped them shut, refusing to cry. I pulled away from Mrs. Shirm and her "poor dear girl" sympathy.

"Amelia has told me about your father's drinking problem," Mrs. Shirm continued. "So many men are lured into the evils of the saloon. That's why we're working to close them down. May we sit and talk a bit?"

We sat in the rockers. Mrs. Shirm leaned toward me.

"My daughter said you couldn't live with your father because of his drinking, so I wondered if you had plans to live with other relatives? If not, I have a friend in New York City who's looking for a live-in nanny for her baby girl. Ideally, she'd like someone a year or two older than you, but I've heard people who've eaten at this tea room say that you're a quiet young lady and extremely hard-working." She paused. I said nothing.

"I was wondering," she continued, "if I could recommend you to my friend? I don't want to bother her if you already have other plans."

"My plan," I said in a strangled voice, "was to live with Mama in the city!" I rocked furiously, then calmed a bit. Amelia and her mother were only trying to help. I could be a nanny. I'd probably live in a nice house too.

As if she read my thoughts, Mrs. Shirm said, "My friend lives in the upper east side. I imagine you would sleep in the lovely nursery with the baby. This really is a wonderful opportunity. There won't be that many for a girl in your...position."

"I don't know what to say," I said. "My Grandpa just asked me live here with him and Mrs. Lewis."

"Really?" exclaimed Mrs. Shirm. Her eyes opened wide. "Your Grandfather and Mrs. Lewis live together?"

"Or, I might do charity work in a settlement house in New York City," I rushed on. "But I have nowhere to live in the city." I paused. Why did Mrs. Shirm look so alarmed? Had I said something wrong? "I'm sorry if I misspoke. I'm so confused."

Mrs. Shirm stood up briskly. "I totally understand," she said. "You have quite a burden. Here's my calling card. Good-bye. Come along, Amelia."

My restless thoughts led me to the boardwalk, and my feet brought me straight to the Angel of Victory statue. Something about it was different today. It wasn't about fallen soldiers. It didn't celebrate victory. Or even Molly Pitcher. Suddenly I got it—today the statue represented Mama! My very own angel. Heavenly. Eternal. Here and everywhere.

"Mama," I whispered. "What should I do? Live with Grandpa and Mrs. Lewis? Be a nanny in New York City?" I sat down on the grass and leaned against the pedestal. The sun-warmed stone felt comforting against my back.

What happened next is unbelievable, but true. I heard Mama's voice. Her words floated right into my ear. "What do *you* want to do?" the voice asked.

Shocked, I answered out loud. "I want to work in the settlement house and help children like you did, Mama." I studied the statue. It looked the same. Nothing had changed. Except me. The angel made me speak the truth. Goosebumps prickled up my arms. More goosebumps from God? I decided to write to Alice Paul.

CHAPTER TWELVE

Thornley and Thammy

Tiny Thornley Chapel

Mrs. Lewis brought Grandpa outside to rest on the porch after tea, and I ran into her apartment. My satchel still leaned against the couch. I put the nearly-empty bottle of sherry back in the cabinet, and decided to confess my crime to Mrs. Lewis when we were alone. And promise her I'd never drink her sherry again.

I started my letter to Miss Paul a few times, but couldn't finish it. Writing the actual words that said Mama had died was just too painful. Two days passed, and still I procrastinated. One afternoon I sat on a lawn chair outside Britannia, watching the Rough Riders. Their singing and marching were perfect. Sam was there in his wheel chair. His sister sat on his lap. He waved, and rolled toward me.

"Hi, Elsie," he said. "This is my sister, Sarah. This is Elsie, Sarah. Say hello."

"Hello, Elsie," she said. "I have two teeth loose. Want to see?" She wiggled her top front baby teeth.

"Two teeth at once!" I exclaimed. "The tooth fairy will be very busy."

"Sarah," said Sam, "go play for a minute. Stay where I can see you."

"All right, Sammy. I'll smell all the flowers in this garden. No bees, I hope."

"She's adorable, Sam," I said. "Look at those curls bounce. I'd give anything to have hair like that."

"What's the matter with your own hair?" he asked. "It's perfectly fine." Speechless, I blushed. Seconds ticked by.

"Elsie, I'm very, very sorry about your mother," Sam said softly. "I...I don't know what else to say. I keep seeing you and her walking with the suffragists in the baby parade. Wearing those yellow banners. I'd never seen you smile so much. Who'd ever think this could happen?"

"That's how Grandpa told me to remember her—at the parade. We were so, so happy that day. I'll never forget it." I struggled against tears, and Sam was quiet. Comfortably quiet. His eyes were the only distraction. Their blueness invited me to dive in and swim around, deeper and deeper.

"You know, I thought my summer was stinky when cousin Teddy came to visit," Sam said. "Or when my little sister tagged along with us. Or when I broke my leg. But nothing compares to your summer. What will you do when it ends?" I told him about living in Ocean Grove with Grandpa and Mrs. Lewis, or in New York City as a nanny.

"What about school?" he asked. "You can't go to school and be a nanny. That's an all-day job." I'd never thought of that. I decided to open my heart.

"What I'd really, really like to do is work at the New York College Settlement House," I said, "and help poor immigrant children. But I guess I still wouldn't have time for school. And I've got no place to live in the city. Our apartment's gone." Sam listened so quietly, I found myself telling him Mama's secret.

"That's incredible," he said. "Sewing baby clothes in the middle of the night. Your mother is quite an inspiration. That must be where you get your strength."

My strength? Sam saw me as strong, not a poor little mouse at all!

"Here's my address," he said, handing me a slip of paper. "I'm up on 88th Street." He looked down at his shoes. "Just in case you...um, decide to write me a letter."

"Yes, I mean, thanks, that is...well, I'd better go check on Grandpa." Sam called Sarah, and I waved good-bye to them both, my heart feeling lighter than it had in days. Light as...nothing. Just light.

"Letter for you," announced Ingeborg when I walked in Britannia. The return address was New York College Settlement House. I tore it open.

My Dear Miss Shaw,

I feel as if I know you already, although we've never met. Miss Glockenspiel told us she spoke at your mother's funeral. I'm sorry to say I didn't know your mother, but I'd heard of the woman who sewed beautiful clothes for our babies. I never put her name together with yours, even when I heard about the terrible fire. When Miss Glockenspiel mentioned your name, I finally put it all together. I'm so, so sorry for your loss.

I'm also concerned about your future. I remember you left your father. Do you have other family to live with? If you need a place, you may live in our dormitory. And we'd love to have you work here. You must go to school, that's important. You'd work after classes and on weekends. I believe we can even pay you a small hourly sum now that you're on your own. We can use you as soon as possible. Summer is a busy time at Ellis Island, and we're swamped here on Rivington Street with immigrants.

Please write and tell me your decision, whatever it may be. My prayers are with you at this sad time.

With sympathy and love,
Miss Alice Paul

Bumbershoot! I could live *and* work at the settlement house *and* go to school! My old school. Molly and I could still be friends! "Yes, yes, Miss Alice Paul," I said aloud, "I accept your offer!" I rushed to Mrs. Lewis's apartment and read the letter.

"But what about living here with us?" Grandpa said,

frowning. "I thought it was all settled. You'd have your own bedroom. Wouldn't you like that?"

"Of course I would, Grandpa, but..."

"Gunther, now don't be getting your knickers in a twist," boomed Mrs. Lewis. "Listen to your granddaughter. She's looking for an opportunity to grow. To work with educated, progressive women. To help others less fortunate. Think about it."

"I guess you're right, Maude," he said. "This is a new 20th century, that's for sure. Women folk didn't trot off alone to work in big cities when I was young. Elsie, you must promise me that if you don't like it at the settlement house, for any reason, you'll come back here. Promise?"

"I do, Grandpa."

"Oh, speaking of 'I do's,' tell her about Friday, Gunther," prodded Mrs. Lewis.

"Friday?"

"You know, Thornley Chapel."

"Oh, dear, of course—Thornley Chapel. Elsie, we're getting married in the chapel this Friday. A few of Maude's nieces and nephews are coming, and you and me, and the staff at Britannia."

"I've closed the tea room all day Friday," Mrs. Lewis said. "No explanation, just a closed sign. We'll eat there after the ceremony. A simple lunch, no fuss. I'm sure tongues will wag anyway, marrying so soon after a death in the family. But we know how deep our sadness is, and how much we mourn your dear mother."

"She's right, of course," Grandpa said. "But with you leaving soon, Elsie, it's just one more reason to marry now. I want you at the ceremony. I've asked a minister friend to officiate, and told him not to tell my tent neighbors. We want a small, quiet service."

After supper, I slipped away to write to Alice Paul, accepting her offer. I would arrive on Saturday, I told her. Everything seemed to be happening quickly. Mrs. Lewis's family came by train late Thursday. Friday morning her niece appeared in a lovely white tea dress. She offered me another one she'd brought along, but I said no. Mama's handmade black skirt and shirtwaist fit my mood. I looked in the mirror. My waist looked a little thick. Should I borrow a corset? I heard Mama chuckling in my head and saying, "Told you so!" I decided to forego the corset this time. I pinned the faded pink rosebud from her funeral over my heart.

Mrs. Lewis called me down to her apartment. She laid a strand of pearls around my neck and latched it. "You're like a granddaughter to me," she whispered in my ear, "and I'm giving you this in remembrance of your Mama on this bittersweet day. I hope you'll accept it." I gaped in the mirror, stunned at the beautiful pearls.

"I...I don't know what to say," I stammered. "I've never had such a lovely gift." My heart welled up, and I blurted out the guilty words bursting to be heard. "I'm so sorry about drinking your sherry, Mrs. Lewis. And I ...."

"Blimey, child. No talk of that now," she said. "I figured it out awhile ago. Ta' for telling me the truth, but you have a bigger problem than taking one bottle. A problem that could ruin your life. But we'll talk about that another time. Oh, and ta' means thanks, in case you're wondering."

"Ta' to you too," I said, trying to hug the width of her.

"Ta' so much."

"All right, then," she said, wiping her eye, "skedaddle while I get into my dress. Here it is. Do you like the gray satin?"

"Oh, it's beautiful," I said.

"I'm not wearing white, Lord knows," she sighed, "but I won't be married in mourning black either."

Tiny Thornley Chapel was a block south of the Great Auditorium. It was built in memory of a long-time Sunday School teacher, and everything inside was child-sized—the perfect place for a small wedding. Like Patience, the pews were petite. She sat with Philip in the second row, her feet barely skimming the ground. Behind them sat more staff members, all dressed in their finest. Not an apron in sight. Hank and Sally walked in wearing beautiful suits and hats, looking as if they'd just left the Easter parade. They slid quietly into seats in the back row. I joined the Lewis family in front.

Sun streamed through the narrow stained glass windows. Britannia roses decorated the altar. The pump organ played softly as Mrs. Lewis marched up the aisle. Her silvery dress had puffy sleeves that accentuated her roundness. She wore a small gray hat with white feathers and carried a bouquet of white roses. Grandpa looked pinched and hot in a tight-fitting black suit. He leaned heavily on his cane. A white rosebud was pinned to his lapel.

The ceremony was short, but so sweet. The minister spoke of the special circumstances of this wedding, and the hope it gave our families in a time of great sadness. Rings were exchanged. I wondered if they were old rings being used again, or new ones, but it didn't matter. Nothing mattered but the bride and groom's smiling faces. The small room grew brighter and brighter. It felt like Mama's love shining down a blessing. Shining like starlight at noon—invisible to the eye, but still there.

Wait! "Mama, did you hear that?" I whispered as the organ played. "Love, like starlight at noon? I'll write you a poem yet."

Grandpa pulled me aside after the wedding luncheon. "I know you're leaving tomorrow, Elsie. I won't be able to walk to the train with you, so here's money to buy your ticket. And money for the trolley and any necessities."

"Thank you, Grandpa. I was planning to use the money I earned this summer, but now I can save that. May I go to your tent and get my envelopes?"

"Yes, yes, of course. And please take your rosemaling box." He cleared his throat several times. "Well," he said finally, "we're coming to visit you in the fall, soon as the summer season ends. I'm corresponding with J.P. Morgan Bank, and arranging for your mother's bank account to be switched to your name."

"You should keep that, Grandpa."

"No, no. My daughter saved it for an apartment for both of you. I hope you'll use it for your own place someday. You're growing up mighty fast, Elsie," he said. "Just be careful and stay away from your father. As long as he's drinking, he can't be trusted."

I was leaving Grandpa's tent when I heard a girl's voice. "Thammy, there'th Elthie." It was Sarah, her wide open smile showing a gap where two front teeth should be. I put down my satchel, and held out my arms. She ran into them with the trusting instincts of the very young.

"Hello, Sarah," I said with a laugh. "What happened to your teeth?"

"One fell out, and one wiggled and wiggled. Papa pulled it out. It hurt!"

"Oh, poor Sarah. Say your brother's name again."

"Thammy, Thammy, Thammy," she sang. Sam and I laughed together.

"I was hoping to see you, Thammy," I teased. "I've made a decision and here's my address. I'll be living and working at the settlement house *and* going to school!"

"That's wonderful, Elsie! I've heard a lot about your family lately. Everyone feels terrible about your mother, of course, but then I heard Mrs. Shirm tell my mother that your Grandfather and Mrs. Lewis were living in sin."

"What? Living in sin? Where did they get that idea?"

"Mrs. Shirm said you told her they were living together," said Sam. "And everyone knows they're not married."

"I told her no such thing! All I said was I might live at Britannia with Grandpa and Mrs...oh. No one knew they were getting married. Shows how nasty rumors start. Well, they were married this very day in Thornley Chapel. I hope everyone hears that!"

"Is that why you look so pretty today?" Sam asked. I blushed. "Enough about stinky gossip," he said. "Want to take a walk?"

"Yes, I'd like that."

"Sarah, run back to our tent like a good girl. Mother's there. I'll be back later."

"I don't think your mother likes me," I said shyly, walking beside his wheel chair.

"I noticed that too," Sam said, "but it changed after the parade. She heard about the marching suffragists and how you and your mother joined in. My parents are very progressive. They believe in women voting. She thought you were brave."

"I didn't see her at the parade. Or your famous Teddy."

"Sarah was sick and Mother stayed home with her. And Teddy left Ocean Grove before the parade. His mother had a baby girl and he was needed at home. It was stinky. Stinky he had to leave, that is, not that he had a baby sister."

Sam laid my satchel on his lap. We traveled the length of the boardwalk, from Asbury Park to Bradley Beach and back again. I told him I was leaving tomorrow. He seemed surprised it was so soon. The sky did its twilight ballet of pink and blue and gold. My favorite time of day with my new favorite person.

"I'm glad to go back to New York City," I said, "but I'm going to miss all this open space and fresh air." And you, I said silently.

The next morning I cleared tables for the last time and emptied my bedroom. Mrs. Lewis gave me a carpet bag for my clothes. I rested my cheek a long time against Grandpa's beard.

"Blimey, I hate good-byes," said a sniffling Mrs. Lewis. "Don't forget we're coming to see you. And write to us. Here's Britannia stationery, so there's no excuse." The whole staff stood on the porch waving good-bye. Kerry ran down the stairs.

"I'm walking to the station with ya," she said. We hadn't spoken much since the funeral. Even at the wedding. Maybe she was afraid I'd cry. Or she'd cry. She looked like she was going to right now.

"I'm gonna miss you something awful, Elsie," she said, bursting into tears.

"You are? I didn't think you even liked me. I told you I'll be at the College Settlement House on Rivington Street. The lower east side. Come visit. Summer ends pretty soon. Have you decided what to do?"

"Well, Mrs. Lewis, er, Mrs. Heines as she wants to be called now, just asked me to stay here year-round. She closes down the guest rooms and tea room, but it's still a big house. She wants me to clean and run errands."

"That's great, Kerry! You know, you've changed a lot the last few weeks. Mrs. Lew…I mean, Mrs. Heines feels she can trust you now. I was worried about Grandpa and her rattling around in that big old house. I feel so much better knowing you'll be there. Oh-oh, people are starting to board the train." I ran to buy my ticket. When I returned, Kerry was fighting tears again.

"Elsie, this is for you," she said, putting a dime and nickel in my hand.

"I'm sorry I stole your pay that first week. I'll never do it again, to anyone!" I dropped the coins in my pocket. "Elsie?" she continued. "I want you to know I went to church that day you asked me. I stood way in the back, near a door. I heard the preacher. I'm being careful now. I won't end up like Kathleen."

"That's wonderful," I said, squeezing her tightly. "I'll see you when I come to visit." Kerry walked back to the bridge, and there, rolling toward me, was Sam!

"I went to Britannia," he said, "and they told me you'd already left. Hold on." He lifted his cast and set it on the ground. Pushing up on his good leg, he reached for me. I stepped into his arms, my heart thumping. I never wanted to leave, but he immediately stepped back.

"I thought of something last night," Sam said. "You know those underground trains they're building in New York? Soon we'll be able to get around the whole city in the blink of an eye. No traffic, no trolleys. I'll come visit, if it's all right with you. I might not even wait for the tunnel trains."

"That would be nice, Sam. Real nice. Write and let me know." We stood, staring at each other. Was he going to kiss me? I turned my head slightly, my cheek facing him. I closed my eyes.

"This is stinky!" he said loudly. My eyes flew open. "The stinkiest thing ever! Why do you have to leave, anyway?" He stomped his good foot on the ground, like a two-year-old having a tantrum. I sighed. Kisses would have to wait for the future.

"All aboard!" called the conductor. "All aboard for New York City."

I ran to the train, hopped aboard and found a seat. Sam and I waved until the train left the station. I fingered my ticket. It still said, "Good for One Passage This Day and This Train Only." On the last trip with Mama, I thought those words meant the end of everything I knew. But it was only the beginning. Could it be that endings are really only new beginnings?

Sam's comment about the underground train reminded me of Father and how hard he worked, digging in the pits. How he came home tired, covered in sweat and dirt. I rummaged in my satchel and found the temperance pledges. I'll find you, Father, I vowed. I'll find you and help you sign this pledge, no matter how long it takes. The other pledge, I now knew, was for me. I had a craving for drink, just as Father did. When he signed his pledge, I'd sign mine. And we'd be family again. A broken family without Mama, but still family.

Something yellow gleamed in my satchel—the suffrage banner. I pulled it out and ran my fingers over the white letters, "Votes for Women." Maybe I'd go to a suffrage meeting with Minnie.

I laid back against the headrest and closed my eyes. Every memory of Mama this summer played through my head. Good times and bad times. Tears trickled from my closed eyelids. My head rolled, swaying with the train. I thought I would sleep, but instead I pulled out a piece of stationery and started writing. Before long, words had taken shape on the page. Miraculous words that rhymed! They just came out that way, one word after another.

M a m a   a n d   M e

We rode the train
To escape our pain
Then walked by the sea,
My Mama and me.

But we couldn't escape
The fire's sad fate
That tore us apart
And broke my poor heart.

Bumbershoot! I'd written a real poem! Do you hear me, Mama? Do you like the poem? Don't worry, the next one will be better. I promise.

THE END

Resources

BOOKS

Bell, Wayne T., *Images of America: OCEAN GROVE,* Arcadia, 2000

Bell, Wayne T. and Flynn, Christopher M., *Ocean Grove in Vintage Postcards,* Arcadia, 2004

Daniels, Morris S., *The Story of Ocean Grove, Golden Jubilee 1869-1919,* The Methodist Book Concern, 1919

Dolkart, Andrew S., *Biography of a Tenement House in New York City: An Architectural History of 97 Orchard Street,* The Center for American Places, 2007

Gourley, Catherine, *Gibson Girls and Suffragists,* 21st Century Books, 2008

Laskey, Kathryn, *A Time for Courage: The Suffragette Diary of Kathleen Bowen* (Dear America Series), Scholastic, 2002

May, Ernest R. and Editors, *The LIFE History of the United States, Vol. 9: 1901-1917 "The Progressive Era,"* TIME-LIFE Books, 1976

McGovern, Ann, *If You Lived 100 Years Ago,* Scholastic, 1999

Ocean Grove Camp Meeting Association Annual Reports 1904, 1905, 1906, Published by the Association each year

Pike, Helen-Chantal, *Images of America: Asbury Park,* Arcadia, 1997

Walton, Mary, *A WOMAN'S CRUSADE: Alice Paul and the Battle for the Ballot,* Palgrave Macmillan, 2010

Wolff, Daniel, *4th of July, Asbury Park: A History of the Promised Land,* Bloomsbury, 2005

NEWSPAPER AND EXHIBITS

Asbury Park Daily Press, Aug. 20, 1887, *"Summer in the Tents of O.G."*

Historical Society of Ocean Grove, Exhibit and Timeline, *Carrying the Torch: Ocean Grove and the Fight for Woman's Suffrage,* 2007

Lower East Side Tenement Museum, 108 Orchard Street, New York, New York